A MANOR FOR A TREASURE HUNT

SURAJ SHETTY

Made with ♥ on the Notion Press Platform
www.notionpress.com

Dedicated to my parents and family,

And to

The ever-inspiring Ruskin Bond

Contents

CHAPTER ONE

He would arrive in Mangaluru on Saturday early morning after taking a late night flight from Delhi on Friday. It was a dreary routine, having to leave home for the airport by 9.30 PM and eventually reaching final destination by 6 AM the next morning. He bore through this run because he got to enjoy the 3AM stopover at Bengaluru airport.

Another reason being, the Red-Eye flights were quite friendly to the pocket; especially his, being a lighter one.

Taking off from Delhi at around 12.15AM, Uttaran braced for the jerky take-off as he looked out the window at the runway asphalt rushing by. He leaned back into his seat just as the plane took wing and nosed up. He would have to wait for the few anxious seconds when the jet would powerfully lug upwards and curve to the left while gaining altitude, vibrating hard as it pulled through and finally levelled to a horizontal. This was the part when he felt smoggy in his head, for the few seconds when as if his brain was being pudding-nudged inside. The plane finally stabilised to a normal and all the loud rumbling noises had gradually subsided with a submissive long creak. His air-filled ears popped a couple of times as he gulped, and he was now ready to open a book, feeling light headed and ready to go. He could never sleep through a flight, and the warm coffee refills, though expectedly bland and tasteless, helped in finishing a breezy novella by the end of the flight.

The Red-Eye, presumed to be so called because a midnight flight was known to induce restlessness and thus resulting in a sleepless red eye, finally landed at a twinkling Bengaluru at 2.45AM.

Uttaran would have a full two and a half hours prior to his connecting flight from Bengaluru to Mangaluru. He would first visit the 24x7 open South Indian Restaurant housed at the far end of the airport's vast and expansive intra shopping lounge. All stores except the few eateries were closed at this hour of night. With a leisurely stroll he perused some of the displays in the open-air store spaces prohibiting entry, sealed only by the bright-red retractable barrier strap belt. The Restaurant, at this hour, would be completely free and have no crowding at all. He would order his favourite cup of masala spiced tea along with a plate of steaming Idli and Sambar while enjoying the scenes around.

Some guests, mainly the young professionals, were finger-tapping away at their laptops diligently even at this unearthly hour. And some others were gently swaying their heads, their earphones plugged in and thinly wires snaking to their mobile phones.

Not so unearthly, actually, inside the airport.

The airport was a life universe of its own, perpetually daylight with all the bright white lights on the high roofs and columns in the expansive lounges, cheery potted plants lively and flowering with a spectrum of colours, charging the whole ambience alive. The large TV screens placed intermittently between every few rows played sports entertainment non-stop, giving a sense of a buzzing newsroom studio even in the midst of dozy passengers. The floating aroma from the eateries, the mix of people young and old, and the airport ground staff scattered all around gave the airport a life of its own. The cacophony never dulled even for a fleeting moment.

Some of the more exhausted ones helped themselves to the neighbouring vacant seats by stretching long, while a few couples were engaged in conversation. The kitchen staff at the eatery was up and about even at this hour, cheerfully going about their mundane routines of whipping up the most delicious of snacks, as if in the sure knowledge that the restaurant was soon going to be brimming with crowds to clean-sweep their delicacies.

By the time Uttaran was done with his midnight breakfast and a second cup of tea, the announcement for boarding commence could be heard, as if on cue. He walked over to his departure gate which was located a floor down below the shopping lounge. He let the queue for boarding shorten a bit and finally came up behind, the last one.

It was a small size aircraft with seating for about a hundred passengers. The short-duration flight from Bengaluru to Mangaluru took no time at all, and by the time in-flight tea and snacks were about done, the landing would have commenced. There was no time for a book here.

The flight landed at 6AM, and after a quick retrieve of his bag from the conveyor belt, he booked a cab at the pre-paid taxi counter located at the sole exit gate of the airport. The drive from the airport to his native home took an hour at the most. Uttaran would be home just in time to join his parents for breakfast.

The cab sped through the empty roads of the quaint little villages lined with rice paddy fields on both sides of the drive, and cows grazing on the scattered patches of grass by the roadside. An occasional petty shop would show up in between a sudden spurt of thatched village houses lined a few metres away from the main road, and one could see a few village locals sipping their morning tea, all huddled together on a couple of benches outside.

The village scenery outside was enchanting. Alongside, little snippets and anecdotes from the cab driver regarding recent happenings and developments in the villages and towns they passed by seemed to uplift his mood further.

Uttaran had been visiting his ancestral home ever since his childhood days, when he came over during his school breaks and vacations. That was also the time for the band of cousins, young and old, who travelled from various corners of the country, near and distant, and got together at the ancestral home to have the time of their lives. The memories of playing games, foraging and gruelling for ripening seasonal fruits on the trees and on the grounds, ventures of afternoon treks through the lush green paddy fields and out into the widespread plantations of coconut and areca nut trees, having food together while seated down cross-legged on the kitchen floor, with Grandma's delectable recipes being dished out on fresh green banana leaves...they all came rushing back mingling with the light morning breeze that ruffled Uttaran's mane through the open window of the speeding cab.

And now, they were just that-memories. Reminiscences of the times gone by. Some of the gang of cousins were in touch, but most were not. They had all moved on with their busy lives, having to manage the hectic mix of family and profession, though not necessarily in that order. It was perfectly understandable. The rare moments of joyous reunions and meetings would occur on some grand occasion of marriage of a cousin, (some arranged, but mostly the union of a love affair, given the times), and there would be this relentless burst of exhilarating chatter and rolling banter amongst all of them.

Strangely, as he got older, the urge to be closer to his native village and amongst his family relatives and cousins seemed to become even more profound.

It had been a couple of years since Uttaran's parents had relocated to the ancestral house. And ever since, not only Uttaran, but also his younger sister Suma, had been regularly visiting the parents every two or three months. It would ideally be a five day break extending into the weekend, and it did not interfere too much with his office work routine as senior employees in the firm had been offered a flexible work-from-home alternate, as long as work productivity and performance did not suffer. Uttaran made sure he fully utilised this official privilege to the maximum. The frequent trips to the village home and experiencing first-hand the sleepy and unhurried pace of the village life had ingrained in him now a deep yearning for a similar lifestyle.

Also, there was another motive.

For some time now, Uttaran had a few musings going through his mind. No, none to do with his work. This was something about the ancestral home that had piqued his curious mind. Something to do with a probable hidden treasure. Right there, at the native home. It was just a theory for now. His very own.

As he had got older, Uttaran had begun to ponder about the history of the ancestral home. There were many questions buzzing around in his head.

The mansion was indeed a marvel. They, the present generation, had all taken it for granted as they had gained it by easy inheritance. The grandeur of it all had been lost on all of them. But he remembered how, when guests visited the home for the very first time, would stop and stare in awe at its expansive magnificence as they slowly walked up the first flight of stairs. How did it ever come to be? Who had built it? How old was it? How was the secluded spot for building the house determined?

How did it end up finally coming to be their ancestral home...despite the fact there being multiple lineages of descendants? He began to enquire these various matters and details, trivial and otherwise, with his mother. He assumed she would be aware of its detailed history.

When he had been younger, all of this never mattered. But now, he was suddenly curious about everything. His mother, along with her siblings (five in all) was descendant fifth in line, as joint inheritors of this vast expanse of an estate. Her Great Grandmother's maternal Uncle had built this grand manor-like estate, with a massive palatial residence surrounded by farmlands and green plantations spreading out in all direction in acres, far beyond the eyes could see, and finally stopping short at the foot of the surrounding hillocks. The inheritance of property followed a matrilineal rule, and thus eventually, Uttaran's Grandmother, being a single child to her parents, by sheer destiny had inherited the entire estate. And after her, Uttaran's mother and her siblings finally ended up to be combined and joint owners of this grand estate that included the mansion they presently resided in.

Uttaran's cab finally reached home. He did not have too much luggage, just a single bag. He never needed much for an extended weekend. Besides, his clothings were already stocked in a cupboard in a room upstairs, ever since the times he had been frequently visiting home and this decision came very handy. He could always travel light.

The parents were out in the sitting room, right opposite the main entrance and across the open central courtyard. Father was sitting on the sofa, hunched slightly over the morning newspaper while Mother was listening to the morning radio that was playing some old movie song. They looked up and smiled as soon as he entered the main, large imposing doorway to the huge residential expanse. Uttaran greeted his father and smilingly gave a bear hug to his mother, and the three of them, chatting, went inside to the dining room to have breakfast.

'You are early' Mother said, while serving hot crispy white Dosas freshly prepared and kept in the hot box.

Uttaran was helping himself to the coconut chutney, a favourite companion whenever Dosas were made for breakfast. 'It is the exact regular time Ma. Neither late nor early. The flight was right on schedule.'

Father generally enquired about office work and Uttaran replied with the same monotonous answers, that everything was routine and nothing out of the ordinary.

'Why don't you come with me to Delhi? Just for a few days. It would be a nice change.'

'But we cannot. Not at this time of the year' Mother replied. 'The paddy fields are just about ready to be harvested in a couple of weeks and then, the fields need to be cleared all clean and prepared for the next round of crops before the monsoons arrive.' Uttaran nodded his head understandingly. 'We need to be here while the harvesting works are undertaken or else..you know how workers are these days..If we leave during this period of the harvest, they would not mind the extra leeway and while away their time at the most crucial junctures. It could damage the whole produce.'

Father interjected 'We will make it once the harvest is completed and done. There will be a couple of free months in between harvest and the oncoming monsoons and we could come over for a week or so.'

The Dosa and coconut Chutney combination was immensely alluring and Uttaran helped himself to a couple more. He did not have the luxury of such delicious options in Bengaluru, where he had to make do with food from restaurants. Not that they were not good, but they were never as tasty as home food cooked by Mother. He fully immersed the torn bits of Dosa into the bowl of the thick, white chutney dotted with black mustard seeds and little green curry leaves, and devoured them with relish.

'Ma, could you tell me more about the Patriarch? Grandma's Great Grand Uncle? Do you have photographs of him, or his family...some old, forgotten album perhaps?'

Mother had finished her breakfast and just about to get up from her seat. 'I remember seeing a few albums kept around somewhere... when I was very young. But I never got to see them again. I don't even recollect going through the albums as I was never too curious. But I am sure your Grandma had kept it someplace safe. You can look for it in the rooms above.'

She had collected the empty plates and walked to the kitchen. Uttaran and Father got up behind her to wash up.

Uttaran had got down to his office routine shortly after breakfast, logging in to his office in Delhi remotely on his Laptop to mark his attendance online. He generally used one of the many rooms upstairs, on the upper storey, where the internet signal penetration was highest, and also because, there would be no disturbances and distractions of small talk with guests who regularly came in to meet the parents.

There were many close relatives who lived in the vicinity, most of them cousins of Uttarans' mother, and family friends who would often drop in for a little chit-chat over a cup of tea and delightful savouries. The parents enjoyed these incoming visits a lot, just the way they visited their near kin and all. Such leisurely and mind-refreshing visits helped everyone in the extended families to keep abreast of all the local happenings within and outside of the families, and was also a source of plain delight when the elders got together and queried about the younger ones in the families: their children, the upcoming marriages, the double-edged thrill of the board exams that some teens were about to endure, the professional prospects of some of the brighter ones, and so on. Uttaran too, delighted in such little gems of get-togethers and banter, but office time now was just that – pure office-work time. He would have time for all of that leisure and more, but later.

Uttaran came down from his room long after lunch break time, and joined his parents who were already at the dining table having lunch. They had their lunch at a fixed time, and never waited for him as they were aware of Uttaran's irregular schedule. Uttaran's time of lunch and dinner were invariably erratic. He had lunch only when he felt deep hunger pangs, a bad habit that he had yet to overcome. There was no definite time slot. The primary reason for this was the innumerable little cups of tea he had throughout the entire day, right from breakfast through lunch, and until dinner time. This routine had played spoilsport with his appetite ever since his college days, when he had got addicted to tea, and apparently the reason for his slim physique that never seemed to plump up.

The Lunch spread was varied, but simple. There was the unpolished red rice, his favourite dal (yellow gram lentils), a dry beans and a ladyfingers side dish, both of which had been lightly fried using grated coconut, and a little of the chicken curry that was a carry-over from the previous day. The parents had already finished their lunch, and Father was resting in the sitting area while Mother decided to give company to Uttaran.

'So, how is everyone?' Uttaran queried, referring to his relatives but not any one in particular.

'Everyone's fine. I do call them all almost everyday' Mother replied. 'All' referred to her brothers and sisters, the close-knit bonding between the siblings apparent in her tone. She always seemed joyous when she mentioned about them and her nephews and nieces, and the affection was mutual. Uttaran remembered how he and his sister Suma, as youngsters during vacations, would always be shifting from one aunts' home to another week by week, town by town, spending time with a separate set of cousins at their respective homes and enjoying all the pamper and love showered by the elders. 'There may be a couple of marriages in the coming couple of months, so let's see.'

'Do you and Papa go visiting?'

'No, not very often. We all do meet when we get together during some occasion or the other that is always happening nearby. Some engagement ceremony, some marriage, or maybe even at the baby showers...something or the other is always happening around here.' she responded with a smile.

Uttaran was helping himself to another round of rice and dal, this time adding a dollop of some thick, white curd on the top.

'Is anyone visiting anytime soon?'

'No..no one in particular. But you know about Ratna..he can drop in anytime. Anywhere. Unannounced' she smiled, referring to her younger brother. Ratnama was the elder of the two brothers amongst the set of five siblings, now retired from work and having settled with his family in Bengaluru.

'Oh yes' Uttaran smiled, remembering how, in the old days gone by, his favourite Uncle would spring up at the most unexpected of times and conjure loads of fun and frolic and light up the entire ambience. He was one of those rare ones who had this very unique and unexplainable quality that was engrossing to both the elders and the younger ones. He had the magic still on, even now. 'Is he coming?'

'We had spoken a couple of days earlier, and he had asked about you and Suma. I had mentioned that you may be visiting, so..you never know. He loves to visit when the nephews and nieces are here.'

'And, is anyone from the gang of cousins visiting?' Uttaran was speaking about his maternal cousins who were also regularly in touch with his parents. The reason was, they would always inform the parents beforehand about their plans prior to travel.

'Shouldn't you know better?' Mother countered, 'You are more in touch with them than we are.'

'I wish we were, but somehow, we don't get the time. Or rather, we don't make the time I guess' he answered plainly. He was still sweeping his plate clean with his fingers, covering every bit of it to get whatever remained of the pale yellow mix of dal and curd. 'Did Suma call?'

'Yes. She calls up every day. Every morning, every afternoon, every evening and every night'. Both Mother and son smiled at this quip. Suma was the favourite of both her parents. While she was doted upon more by her father, but for Suma, it was her mother who was favourite. She had to share everything with her mother who was more like a friend now. 'She may visit this week she said, but not quite sure. It depends on her work schedule. Are you done licking with the plate? I have to clear the table.'

Uttaran smiled, not looking up, and slowly got up from his chair and picked up his plate and a couple of little bowls and carried them to the kitchen. Mother followed him with the remaining items.

'Ma, I will stay upstairs and continue with my office work. Please let me know if you need anything. And please send me a cup of tea around 3.30PM.'

He passed Father who was speaking on the phone, on the way upstairs.

'It's Suma' he said.

Uttaran turned around and gently took the phone. 'Hi Suma. Any plans to visit? I will be here till the weekend.' There was some reply from the other end, and Father could not make anything out. 'We have to try and have this done this time. Uncle too, may be visiting. Please try to make it. You can work from here just as well.' Finally, Uttaran smiled and returned the phone back to Father.

'She may be coming' he said, while going on ahead upstairs to one of the bedrooms to continue with his office work.

It was finally seven in the evening when Uttaran finally logged off from his office and came downstairs to join his parents. He normally worked a couple of extra hours online so that he could compensate for some of the leisure time he liberally took in between office hours whenever he worked from home at his native place. It gave him a partial sense of relief and left him free of guilt that he had not wasted any of his office time. That way, he enjoyed his leisure time even more.

It was beginning to get dark in the evening sky. An aeroplane was flying over in the distance, with its twin lights blinking on and off. Uttaran walked over through the corridor and out into the exteriors where there were two large platforms covering almost the entire floor space, one on either side of the main entrance doorway. It was about three feet high from the floor and completely black on the top and sides, which doubled as a sit-out and also as a sleeping space to accommodate the numerous guests that invaded the mansion on some of the grandest of occasions such as marriages or Puja ceremonies.

Uttaran loved to sit out there and watch the field, lush green and ready for harvest, spread out in front with the tall swaying coconut trees behind in the distance, bordering the field on all sides and spreading even further beyond. The clear night sky with grey floating clouds and the herons gliding back to their homes with their night calls made for a tranquil view. He could see a few workers from the fields returning to their homes while some were heading opposite upslope, to their favourite country liquor shop located on the main road up above.

He reminisced about the earlier attempts to search for the treasure he was so convinced it existed.

CHAPTER TWO

THE NEAR MISSES

Uttaran was determined to make a start to the search for the treasure. He had not been able to visit his native home for a few months now due to a very hectic office schedule. The projects for the team were coming up endlessly and he had to be there personally to guide and supervise his team, and finally to monitor the progress as well as make continual progressive updates and reports promptly, and forward it to his higher office. Any slack in the line of chain would result in irreversible delay in completion and hand over to the client party. Such a delay could be very crucial and in such intensely competitive times, could result in the permanent loss of a very lucrative client account. And entire responsibility for loss of a client account would fall upon the very delicate shoulders of an already burdened Uttaran, the Project Head. And he had three such projects undertaken simultaneously.

Work was always fine with Uttaran, but not with daggers of constantly nagging deadlines dangling over his neck.

Somehow, the urgent projects were finally implemented and handed over. But a flood of other upcoming ones were anticipated soon after. He desperately needed a quick, short break.

It was at this juncture that Uttaran received some news from a cousin. It was about a marriage in the family that had been fixed abruptly and on very short notice, as a very good proposal for another cousin had successfully gone through immediately as soon as feelers had been put out, and prospective talks had begun. It would be a rush visit that Uttaran would have to make to the native home. Uttaran had applied for leave but was not granted any. He had to visit anyway as he made it a point to be present at the weddings of his cousins, no matter how difficult. All of the cousins were a close-knit gang, just like in any family. It was also a great opportunity to catch up with them, and exchange the latest happenings in one anothers' lives. He successfully, though with much difficulty, convinced his skeptical superior that he would work from home and somehow manage his office schedule. Usually, whenever he had to make a visit to the native place, he would always make it appoint to stay for a few more days as the long haul from Delhi to Mangaluru was not worth travelling for just a single day of stay. This time, he would not have that luxury.

Uttaran had been intending to start looking for some hideaway spots and this was the right occasion to begin. He had to start someplace someday, or else he would never begin. Once the marriage occasion and ceremonies were done and over with, and the mansion would be emptied of the guests, he could initially do a reconnaissance of both inside and outside of the mansion. He was not sure where to start. There were so many rooms, ceilings, floor boards inside the vast abode that he would have to scour. He had been procrastinating for a long time now, but soon realised he had to make it work with whatever little spare time he had on hand. Sooner or later, he had to start somewhere.

The marriage ceremony was preceded by a ceremony called the 'Muhurtha' that generally took place two days before the marriage. The 'Muhurtha' is always undertaken at the groom's ancestral home. It is a ritual that has all the elders of the family extending their blessings to the groom, or bride as the case may be, before the auspicious occasion of marriage. The groom is dressed up in traditional ceremonious attire and is seated on a chair that is set on a platform which is florally and colourfully decorated. The few elder ladies of the family then carry out the auspicious puja for the groom and bless him one by one, while applying the sacred tilak on his forehead. This is followed by all the other members of the close family taking their turn to bless the groom. The 'Muhurtha' is finally followed by a grand lunch affair.

A beautiful shamiana had been set up for the occasion in the open courtyard where the guests could sit and have their lunch, which was usually a buffet, protected and shaded from the summer sun. Though purely vegetarian, the spread was varied and delicious.

Once the grand feast was over, the guests, all close members of the extended family, got together mingling in various groups and enjoyed light banter amongst themselves. Refreshing cool drinks were continually served by a few of the workers who had been called upon, to help in setting up the grand luncheon arrangements for the occasion. Finally, around evening time, while a handful of guests decided to stay back at the mansion, most of them decided to head back to their respective homes and planned to meet up again on the day of marriage.

The next day was a leisurely one for the family. There was a day to spare before the big wedding. While the ladies, that is Mother, Suma and a couple of aunts who had decided to stay back, had plans to go out shopping in the city, the gents had no particular plan and had planned to make a casual trip to the town. Uttaran had a whole day to himself.

He first decided to take an update about the progress in works from his subordinate. Thankfully, the office routine was running just fine and the team was managing perfectly. After making doubly sure that his presence online was no more needed, he logged off with a sense of deep relief. He could completely focus on the second priority now.

The mansion was soon empty except for the home workers. Uttaran decided to pursue his course of action without any further delay.

He took a flashlight and entered the storage room, one of the two located on the ground storey, on adjacent sides of the large main hall. He pushed open the heavy wooden door. It creaked a bit as it opened. He kept his head low so as to not hit the thick door frame. It was dark inside. There were no bulbs or lights fitted in the room. Strangely, the room had no electric wiring at all till date. It was as if the mansion residents had completely missed both the storage rooms whenever it was upgradation time for the mansion. The floor, old and dirty, but not dusty, still had the black plastered surface with many portions peeled away to reveal the hard and pitted laterite surface beneath. The walls too displayed the same fate. The room in itself was very small, with a low ceiling and no windows. The wall on the right had a single wooden shelf just a foot below the ceiling, running along the entire span and about a foot in depth. Devoid of any daylight due to its location, the darkness further enhanced the compressing feel of a claustrophobic enclosure. Uttaran treaded in cautiously, fully aware that presence of a scorpion or even a sly rat snake curled and hidden in the night of a dark corner was not uncommon.

He flashed the torch light, darting it all around the room, looking for a probable hiding spot. The room was an ideal location for a stash away. It had another small door at the end of the wall on the left, which opened into another little room, even smaller than the outer room.

In the earlier days , the room had been used as a storage for storing the harvested rice, all filled in gunny sacks once they had been de-husked after a routine session of thrashing and winnowing of the harvested produce. The gunny sacks would be cleanly lined up against the wall in the inner room, barely leaving any space to walk. The bales of hay, which were essentially the leftovers after the de-husking and used as animal feed, were stored in the outer room. The practice was still followed even in the current times, the only difference being in the quantity of stock then and now. The earlier times had seen both the storage rooms being full and bursting with the produce stock, whereas in the present times, the produce was not as much.

The mansion requirements were very comfortably fulfilled by the produce from the fields, and whatever surplus of rice stock that remained, was immediately transported to the rice mills in the vicinity. The rice mill proprietors were ready buyers always looking to purchase the surplus produce from the farmlands and process them for quality, before having them packed and sealed and selling the entire quantum stock to the local wholesalers.

Uttaran was looking for some sort of a hatch or a sign of an opening or recess. He looked at the floor, and then the walls around. He finally turned the torch light up, to the wooden-beamed ceiling, darting it to and fro along its width. Nothing. It was too dark to be noticeable, even if it had been there.

He entered the inner room. The inner room was even more dark. The black walls, old and plain, were bereft of any cabinets or shelves and seemed to have nothing to hide. He tapped a couple of times on the wall directly in front, barely visible. He looked around again, and quickly turned to come out. Standing solitary in the room, dark and empty and soundless, gave him the shivers.

He darted the flashlight around once again in the outer room, before coming out of the storage. He decided against checking the second such storage room. After this single survey, he had already convinced himself that the storage rooms were not a good idea of a hiding spot.

He closed the heavy door of the storage room. Just adjacent to the stairway to the upper floor was the God's room. Uttaran was half-minded whether he should go inside and try to look around.

The God's room, which housed the sacred and revered deities, had two rooms. The Outer room, big and spacious, had an old wooden cupboard and a big wooden chest. Both very old, but not in damaged condition. Both of the items were polished and maintained well as they housed the materials required to decorate and ornament the revered deities housed in the inner second room. The cupboard and the chest were always kept locked, never to be tampered with by anyone other than the family priest, who was the one and only sole person allowed to bath and clean the revered deities seated on the wooden swings in the inner room. He would then florally and ornamentally decorate the deities and perform the rituals as per the religious norms customarily followed. Such rituals were observed on a couple of auspicious occasions every year when the whole of the extended families, from near and far, would try to congregate for the holy ceremonies.

Uttaran decided to look again for some sort of hideaway spot. He tapped lightly for any hint of hollows in the walls and floor, and darted the flashlight for an invisible or camouflaged hatch in the wooden-beamed ceiling and on the floor. Almost half-heartedly. The rooms had to be cleaned daily, both in the day and evening. Every nook and corner. Also, any slight damage to the room would be promptly attended to and repaired without any delay. Even the floor had been dug out a couple of times and re-floored due to an invasion from a scurry of rats. So, it seemed very unlikely that the Patriarch would have opted for this room as a hideaway.

Well, even if he had decided to, any hidden treasure would have been long gone given the number of times the walls and floors had to be redone. Even the wooden swings on which the deities had been consecrated and seated had been changed a couple of times due to non-repairable wear and damage.

Uttaran decided to take a break. He was seated in the sleeper chair, looking across the courtyard, at the portrait of the Grand Patriarch, hanging at the centre of the wall in the main hall. On a whim, he got up and walked over to the hall, pulled a chair and stood on it to take a closer look at the portrait.

The portrait, a very old one, but still undamaged, showed the details clear and crisp. The Patriarch was seated on the sleeper chair, the very same chair that Uttaran had been seated on just a moment ago. He was sitting erect with both his elbows resting easy on each of the extended arms of the chair, and fingers of both hands clasped together. A red stone ring was prominently visible on the right middle finger. He was bare chested and wearing just a white dhoti. A stole hung from his right shoulder and was resting folded on his lap, and a walking cane stood slanted on one of the extended arms. Even in this simple attire, he looked authoritarian. Maybe it was the turban which gave that effect. He had on a pair of round-shaped thinly rimmed spectacles. With a slightly greying moustache that hung down slightly at the edges, he may have looked a disciplinarian, but his eyes, soft and lightly half-closed, gave away a hint of soft demeanour. In the background was the wall of the main hall where the portrait stayed hung currently, and the chair gleamed with a light brown hue.

Uttaran leaned forward on to the wall and looked at the chair more closely. It was exactly the same, just as it was now. It did not look like the chair had ever been tampered with, or design altered. He slightly heightened himself, balancing on the edge of his toes. He was examining the chair in detail and he saw a very tiny circle, almost a dot, on the base of the rear left leg of the chair. It was not apparent from afar, but if observed closely, the minuscule slip was clearly visible.

It was a simple painting but done with great care and detail. Uttaran mildly wondered whether the portrait itself was hiding something within itself. Maybe in the finely bordered frame, or at the back of it. Or, what if the painting of the portrait itself held some gold? Uttaran looked at the stole that hung crisply on the Patriarch's shoulder. It had a slight golden hued border to it. Could it be that the painting itself held a smearing of gold within it? Uttaran's mind was dancing wildly in all directions with a hundred possibilities. He could not focus clearly. He bent down to look at the name of the painter. It was signed in Kannada in very small font. Though he could understand the spoken dialect, he could neither read nor write the language in written. Suddenly, he felt exhausted and mentally drained. It all seemed pointless. He got down from the chair and walked back wearily to the sitting room and dumped himself into the comfort of the sleeper chair. This was going to be tough and tiringly tedious.

No, he could not let himself be disheartened. Not so quickly. This was just the beginning.

He jolted himself upright. This would take effort and patience, and stubborn determination. After all, this was his first attempt at search. He would have to be mentally prepared for a long and gruelling grind if he was truly serious about his theory. Going about in a mad rush would not be of any help and use.

He could not undertake something like this in between busy schedules. And definitely not while being in the knowledge that any close relative could visit home unannounced. The mission was best undertaken with prudent discretion. He would have to do this again, but in a very leisured space and time.

The men soon returned from the town, and the ladies arrived shortly after. Uttaran decided to hold the search for the time being and decided to continue with it on his next trip back home. It was time to meet the gang of cousins and he was excited at the prospect of meeting all of them the next day on the grand occasion of the wedding.

The treasure was not going anywhere. It could wait. And he had plenty of time.

The wedding had been a grand affair and just like they had all planned, the cousins, young and old, got together and had a jolly time. They were continually engaged in light banter and were occupied mostly at the food and snacks stalls, away from the main hall where the ceremony was taking place. They had seen it all before and except for the groom and the bride and their respective parents, the marriage ceremony routine was extremely monotonous and the youngsters were too impatient to sit through the whole thing. They would all head back to the hall once the guests would proceed to the podium to congratulate and wish the newly wedded couple and head for the lunch buffet. The hall would be near empty by then.

The cousins made most of the little time they got to be together. Some amongst them had decided to go out for a little get together in the afternoon after the wedding and get back in the evening before the reception that was planned for the same night. While some others decided to go back to their hotel rooms and laze around till reception time. Most of the cousins would head back home the very next day itself so as to not miss their respective office and college and school routines. Only a handful would stay back for a couple more days before heading back home. But no matter however short the duration, the getting together was a big lifeline for all of them. The excitement and the memories of them would last a lifetime, and they would all remember these golden moments the next time they gathered together.

Uttaran and Suma, too, had left for their respective home cities the very next day, knowing he would be back soon to continue with the search.

Uttaran was lost deep in his thoughts when he heard Mother calling out to him for dinner. Uttaran got up to go in, once again realising how badly he wanted to stay back here and live the Arcadian life, unhurried and serene calm.

The aroma from the dinner table revitalised him and he went in, smiling. It was just a passing phase and he would get over it yet again once he left for Delhi.

Dinner time was more about chatter and less about the food. The incessant talks were interrupted a few times by a couple of phone calls from chirpy relatives and cousins. The plates and utensils were cleared quickly as the home workers also had to leave for their homes in the premises of the estate. Night time again was consumed by news and gossip regarding the more interesting and controversial members of the extended family. Both the parents were soon exhausted and went off to sleep while Uttaran decided to make himself a hot cup of tea before picking up a book to delve into.

It was early dawn when Uttaran awoke. The pre-dawn wake up calls from the roosters in the shed behind had aroused him. He looked around for his tea flask. There was a little tea left in it. He poured the tea into the upturned cap of the flask. It was still hot and floating soft curls of steam. He took the cup and walked over to the window and looked through between the rusted old vertical iron grills that partly covered the window. He could see the tall green trees and the thick shrubbery in the slopes of the hillock surrounding the back of the mansion. The cowshed was visible just below the window of his room upstairs, and a worker was busy spreading hay for the five cows in the cowshed. They would soon be let out to graze in the fields nearby.

He finished his tea and then decided to go back to bed. He was on leave anyway from today and he did not have to log in. He could partake of some pure blanket bliss for a few more minutes.

He could hear Mother calling out to the domestic home workers. The ladies, three of them, took take care of the cleaning chores of the mansion. Two of them were given clear duties of cleaning the utensils and the upkeep of the mansion, the works of which they managed to divide between themselves. There was the inevitable trivial quibbling amongst them regarding unclear demarcation of their respective duties but matters were always sorted out by the presiding lady of the house. The third one, the eldest amongst the three, was allocated the duty of running the kitchen. She had been a quick and keen learner and the daughters of the house had always encouraged her to learn the food recipes, old and new, which she had a knack of quickly grasping on. Through a bit of trial and error, she usually came up with satisfactory results without having to stir up the patience of the men of the house, which they were clearly short of. Especially in matters of the palate.

On one instance, a very special but volatile male guest, in the midst of an interesting conversation, had abruptly got up to fling a plate full of rice and over-spiced curry but somehow held himself back when he was reminded by his alarmed and embarrassed wife that the cutlery was premium ceramic. He however, could not contain his fury enough, and while setting the delicate ceramic down on the table, flung the steel glass of water. His eruption was now complete.

The three of them, amongst and by themselves, managed the daily domestic affairs of the mansion, with clear instructions laid out and monitoring being subtly followed by Mother. So, even though the mansion was expansive, its' upkeep and maintenance was not too much of a hassle.

Breakfast was ready by the time Uttaran came down from his room upstairs. He went through the morning ablutions and went directly to the dining table where his Mother was waiting.

'Where is Father?' he asked.

'He has gone to town for the weekly groceries and some other items. He will be back shortly, and then, after a while he would be going back again to the bus terminal to pick up Suma.'

'Oh yeah..' Uttaran realised. Suma, his sister, had mentioned the day before over the phone that she would be leaving by the night bus. 'It slipped my mind completely. She had told me that she would be coming.'

Mother got up to go to the kitchen as Uttaran helped himself to the spread on the table. Nothing elaborate, it was Bread and Omelette with tomato ketchup sauce, a nice favourite, some boiled eggs, and a hot cup of tea.

Uttaran finished his breakfast quickly and went out to the little open yard at the back of the mansion where the cow shed and the coop for the chickens were located. The smell was a mix of dried dung and hay, and it felt earthy and familiar. Some of the little chicks had been let out of the coop and they were scrambling everywhere, pecking hard and swift at the tiny rice grains flung on the ground by one of the workers.

He went back into the kitchen, filled up a small cup of tea and came back out and sat on a step, quietly observing the hens go about their routine, chasing one another and scrambling haywire. There was some kind of a mysterious tranquil in silently observing all the chicken chaos around. This was the good life. And the tea tasted real good too.

He finished his tea and got up and told Mother that he would be upstairs for some time. He wanted to finish reading his book from the previous night.

Father had left again shortly after he had arrived from the town with groceries for the week. Suma would be reaching the town's bus terminal and she had called Father if he could come over and have her picked. She had taken the night bus from Bengaluru. It was an overnight journey and Suma should have arrived by six in the morning. But due to an unforeseen delay, the bus had departed late at around 3AM and was re-scheduled to arrive at the destination town by 11AM. The bus had broken down at the very point of departure and the passengers had been asked to remain seated as they were informed that it was just a minor issue. The repairs had taken close to four hours. The passengers had got very agitated by the time the bus finally left for its destination. Suma generally slept through the midnight run but this particular instance, she had been restless and sleepless the entire journey. She had finally called her Father early morning to ask if he could come to pick her up as there would be no buses leaving from the town to her village interiors around the time she would arrive. Buses leaving for the village interiors were infrequent during the late morning hours as there were not many passengers during the off-peak hours. And Suma was too flustered to wait for a bus after an eleven hour torturous ordeal of a sleepless night.

Uttaran had just come down from his room when Father and Suma arrived. She was carrying just a leather bag which held her Laptop and a Duffel bag. She too travelled light as she also had her clothings and other stuff stocked at home here as she used to visit her parents even more often than Uttaran. Though her weekends in the city were regularly slotted for outings with her close friends, she made an effort to visit her parents every two or three weeks. Be it in between the week for a work-from-home routine, or even for a single day when there was an office holiday coming up.

'Hi Suma. Wow. You look..hassled! What happened?'

'Nothing serious. The bus journey was a nightmare.' Suma responded tiringly as she laid the duffel bag on the sofa and slipped the leather bag off her shoulder before finally slumping on the sofa. 'Where's Ma?'

'She's at the back, at the shed. She had called for some electrician to check on the electric motor pump in one of the plantations.'

'So..why did you want me to come over? Why the hurry?' she queried wearily. The tone in her voice wasn't pleasant but Uttaran knew that it was the overnight journey's effects. She would be herself in time. A cup of tea could help perhaps.

'Parvati' he called out to one of the lady workers 'Please make some tea for us and have it sent over.'

'Listen, I have some inkling of where it might be. I had been looking for it in a couple of spots by myself in the mansion itself, but no luck. I have a few ideas for the likely hideaway spots and I needed to discuss them with you. It was an extended weekend coming up and I did not want to waste this opportunity. We have a full three days. That's why the rush.' He paused, before continuing 'I am sorry for the haste. Did you have a hectic schedule coming up back at the office?' His mock concern showed clearly on his face.

'Uttaran, I will have some tea first and then take a short nap if you don't mind, Yea?' she retorted. 'I too, would like to see if something finally shows up with all your theories. But I am too tired now. So..could you please..?' she cut short.

Suma was an attractive young lady, in her mid-twenties, two years younger to Uttaran. She had always been the academically inclined one, but alongside, she pushed herself through all the extra-curricular opportunities at school and college without anyone prodding her. Extrovert by nature, she loved the rush and mad exhilaration of being in the midst of activities. In fact, at school, Uttaran was famously referred to as Suma's brother. No one quite ever knew where she got her temper from, though.

She had been recruited even before she had completed her final semester while pursuing a four year engineering course and she was living her dream life in her favourite city, Bengaluru, working on what she loved most - Computers. It was all the more fun as many of her school and college friends resided in the same city. The icing was that she was very close to her native home location wise, and she could visit her parents in a jiffy if she wanted to, by taking a 45 minute flight to Mangaluru.

Unmarried and single, Suma's weekly scheduled office routine was invariably followed through by a weekend with office colleagues, who also made up her set of friends, mostly filled with visits to the malls and movies, and occasionally rounded off by visits to the outskirts of the city which housed a few country resorts and attractive nature spots for leisurely yet lively trekking. Vibrant and vivacious, the activity of the outdoors was a great pull and acted like a recharging booster for Suma, and it perfectly complemented the city life that she loved so much.

Though Uttaran never mentioned it in explicit terms, he was very proud of his sister. She was not only a favourite of her parents, but also her cousins, young and old, who doted on her.

Another reason for Uttaran calling Suma over before venturing to make any further moves was that he truly valued her opinion and input. He had vaguely mentioned in passing about his theory with Suma a long time ago over the phone, but she had dismissed it callously then. This time, he would surmise clearly and discuss the idea with her and try to rationally deliberate whether the hidden treasure line of thought could even be harboured. If she found the ideas feasible, or even better, if she could provide solution to the mystery of the hideaway spot, then the two of them would discuss the matter further with their parents and Ratna Uncle and then, finally ask for their go-ahead.

Tea had arrived by then and after a quick gulp, Suma retired upstairs for a siesta while Uttaran gave company to his parents while partaking in some casual banter.

It was soon lunch time. The family had gathered for lunch at the dining table and Uttaran was just about to start his lunch when a familiar car honk from outside indicated an arrival.

'That must be Ratna Uncle' he said, pushing back his chair slightly as he got up to go out and check who it was.

Ratna Uncle was his maternal uncle from Bengaluru, his mother's younger brother, and the elder one amongst the two brother siblings. He would often drive down from Bengaluru, the city of his residence, departing early morning without any sort of prior intimation and reach the ancestral home by early afternoon, just in time to have lunch with the parents. He had always been a regular visitor ever since his early retirement. He would arrive one day, stay home for a week, and depart for Bengaluru again one fine early morning. Then again, the following week, he would return to obligingly attend a couple of close friend and family weddings and other such events, meet up with his old regulars in the town, and then again, head back home.

Uncle came up the stairs to the entrance just as Uttaran reached the main doorway. Uttaran greeted his Uncle, who was also equally surprised to see him there, exchanged pleasantries and walked him right away to the dining room. The parents and Suma, pleasantly surprised, greeted Uncle jovially, asking him to join for lunch. Uncle pulled up a chair and jumped right in.

'When did you arrive here, Uttaran and Suma?' he enquired both, as he helped himself to the food on the table.

'I just came in today late morning' Suma answered. 'Uttaran was already here yesterday.'

'Any special reason, or is it just another casual break?'

'Yes, a short break this time Uncle' Uttaran joined in. 'It had been three months since my last visit and I thought it was time for another one.'

Uncle smiled, and continued partaking of the delicious spread of lunch while simultaneously enquiring and making small talk with Uttaran's father. They had both worked for the same enterprise and there was no dearth of news and happenings about the enterprise, current and past, they could not chatter about. It was mainly about the ex-colleagues they commonly knew and were closely acquainted with, most of whom had settled after retirement in the cities close by, and who were constantly in touch. Both siblings and their Mother thoroughly enjoyed listening to their animated conversations about their past reminiscences and the days long gone by.

They all had a leisurely wholesome lunch while reminiscing about the cheerful good old times, and somewhere in between, while still seated at the dining table, it helped an indecisive Suma to finally take the rest of the day off.

The afternoon, though sunny, was not hot. The open and ventilated layout of the mansion along with the central spacious courtyard under the open blue sky helped in keeping an unhindered inflow of breeze fully through, passing by the narrow living room/sit out. The weather was perfect for a discussion. Mother decided to take a nap, and Uttaran, Suma, Father and Uncle got down to exploring theories, yet again, about how such a mansion came to be, in such a remote location deep inside what would have been a thick forested area, around a hundred and fifty years back.

It had been one such lazy afternoon a few months back that Uttaran had chanced upon some interesting information about the Grand Patriarch during a casual conversation with his Uncle.

Ratna Uncle, out of a deep and personal interest, had been known to actively gather information about the past ancestors and their histories, and even tracing their respective current generations from the various lineages branching down the family tree.

Uncle, now retired, but still healthy and robustly active, was a huge fan of socialising and there was no occasion he would miss, be it either in the very close-knit family of siblings, or any such function that was connected to some most remote distant cousin in the expansive and extended family. With a radiant glow and cheerful disposition to go along with, he loved to make and keep acquaintances and made sure that he maintained close connections with each and every one of them.

This interest of his perfectly complemented his other true passion-that of travelling. The travelling bug ensured that Uncle could dutifully and obligingly attend every function and occasion he had committed to, be it in some distant city or some remote village in the interiors. Even during the time when he was working, he would casually catch a night bus from Bengaluru and sleep through the overnight journey, reach destination early next morning, and check in at a budget hotel. He would then have a hearty breakfast and set out to attend and fulfil whatever social commitments he had. It could be a house warming ceremony of a very dear ex-colleague, or it could be an Engagement ceremony, or also the Christmas dinner party at an acquaintances' place. These were fantastic opportunities for him to meet friends, old and new, and also to forge new friendships through the dear old ones that he met. If he were at a grand wedding, he would intuitively grasp the intricacies of the décor and the grandeur and genuinely seek out the details of the decorators and the planners, even the caterers. The information could always come handy in the future. He also made an extra effort to attend the sombre funerary occasions as he deeply felt that one had to be around a bereaved family to show firm support in their time of grief and loss.

He would then finally return to the hotel for a short booster nap, and then make a brief exploratory escapade into the city or town he had arrived at, visiting and enjoying the local milieu, and then promptly head back home by taking a night bus to Bengaluru. He would reach home the next morning, freshen up, have a light breakfast with the family and head straight to office.

This addictive mix of travel and socialising, meeting new people and forging bonds afresh had inadvertently made Uncle somewhat of an expert in deciphering the underlying connections between the various lineages branching down the large and extended family tree of the Grand Patriarch. Gifted with a sharp memory, he would recall instantly the names of the various people he had met months ago, the familial lineages they derived ancestry from, their respective nature of jobs and even the enterprises they were employed at.

Such an uncommon and unique talent also proved to be an invaluable asset when elders in the extended family seeking alliances for their marriageable grown-ups preferred to consult Uncle prior to putting out feelers for the best suitable proposals.

It was this insatiable hunger for meeting new people and querying about their familial backgrounds and history that had led Uncle unknowingly to the Grand Patriarch's very old ancestral paternal home somewhere in the deep interiors of a village, but not too distant from Uttaran's ancestral home.

Uncle had decided to visit the place all by himself, not absolutely sure that the information he had procured was indeed authentic, but keen enough to check on it. It had been a very short outing but most fruitful.

Uncle had half-expected to see the old home gated and under lock-and-key, dilapidated and all deserted, but he was pleasantly surprised when he was greeted by an old couple who still inhabited the house. They had cheerfully welcomed him and offered him tea, even while regaling him with tales of the olden times. Uncle had tried to explain his distant connection to them by relation with the Grand Patriarch. But the aged couple were not able to fully comprehend the connection that Uncle had with them, in terms of common ancestral lineage. Due to lack of time and running on a tight schedule, Uncle could not stay there for long, but thankfully, he had been able to gather some brief information about the Grand Patriarch in his younger days.

This was precisely what had caught Uttaran's attention. Though he had gathered sufficient information about his maternal family lineage descending down from the Patriarch, he had never been able to source and retrieve any documentation, oral and otherwise, regarding the ancestry and birth place of the Patriarch himself. Where was he from originally, the story of his parents and his childhood, and the circumstances of his younger days, but now, after hearing from his Uncle first-hand, he had decided that he would make at least one visit to the ancestral home that Uncle had been to, and try and gather some history pertaining to the lineage of the Patriarch himself.

CHAPTER THREE

THE TRIGGER FOR TREASURE

Many years back, soon after Uttaran had completed his 12th grade in Delhi where his parents resided, Uttaran had decided to, and sought admission to an Engineering college in a town that was very close to his ancestral home. The town was a very well known and reputed education hub. Uttaran had wanted to stay close to his native home and that was part reason for this decision of his. His parents had no objection to this. They were, in fact, pleased knowing that he was very close to home down south, even though he was away from home. Though he had decided to put up in a hostel in a town very close to the college, he would often head home every second weekend to his native home which was just a few kilometres away. Hardly a half an hours' ride by the local bus.

It had been one of those college days when Uttaran would leave from college on a Friday afternoon without returning to the hostel, and head directly to his ancestral home. He would already have a set of clothes tucked in amongst his college books. He would catch a bus from college opposite in direction to that of the hostel, to the nearest mini-junction at a nearby village which was a 15 minute ride. At the mini-junction, from where most buses headed towards the main couple of cities in different directions, there were also a few buses that routed deep into the interiors through a few villages, catering to the growing rural population, and would finally reach its destination at the bus terminal of the nearest town at the other end. It took about 40 minutes of a breezy bus ride, passing through enchanting spreads of green paddy fields before Uttaran would reach his village bus stop.

Uttaran would walk from the bus stop down the stretch of tar road that sloped in a soft gradient that was a kilometre or so long, with a couple of hair-pin bends and a scatter of cashew and jamun trees on one side of the road. With a song on his lips, he would jingle down the empty road while making sure no one was watching, secretly hoping to encounter a rat snake slithering into the shade of the thick growth of shrubs on the edges of the road. There were autorickshaws at the bus stop that took passengers up and down the slope for a nominal fee, but the walk was so much more invigorating and refreshing.

The slope would finally level about 200 metres prior to the entrance way to his ancestral home. A slip road led away from the main road to take one towards the landmark stones at a dead end, and further right to the main stairway leading up to the entrance of the mansion.

As Uttaran walked up the flight of stairs, he saw a bustle of activity near the stairs. There were some people, all unknown and strangers, who were setting up rows of hanging wires and bright lights. There were a couple of step ladders kept standing in the sides. He passed the doorway and saw some more people who had gathered in the courtyard, all busily scrambling and setting up huge electrical lights and other equipment. A member was shouting instructions while a few others were sitting patiently in the main hall, all dressed up and ready.

It was a TV serial shoot, and Uttaran was just in time for a view.

Uttaran stepped down into the courtyard and walked across, trying to avoid stepping on the wires and knocking over the equipment strewn all around, and came up on the other side by the short flight of steps that led into the open sitting room.

Ratna Uncle, seated in the living room, signalled him to come over while watching the proceedings with curious interest. A shoot was always nice to watch, a nice distraction from the routine banalities. The actors and actresses, also the child actor were all familiar faces. Uttaran had seen them on television in a couple of serials that played daily.

The slight craze for watching live shoots became ingrained when he, as a child, visited the lesser known town of Agumbe located high in the Western Ghats to witness shoot for the very popular MALGUDI DAYS. The entire town would be abuzz live with the hectic schedules of continual shooting of the episodes, and one could sense the setting that was charged and electric.

Though Uttaran could not read or write the local dialect, he could mostly comprehend the oral communication and could also speak, albeit in broken language. Uttaran enjoyed watching the serials with his friends during his dinner time at the hostel mess, at times prodding his friends to explain to him what the proceedings were all about, so that he was in sync with the ongoings in the daily series.

Uttaran enquired with his Uncle about the present shoot that was about to commence shortly. His Uncle explained that the sequence being presently set up for shoot was part of a couple of pilot episodes for a new series, yet to be aired. The story was about a prestigious joint family that lived in a village, descendants to an erstwhile landlord and how their lives get disrupted and disjointed when they are made aware of a possible treasure, allegedly hidden somewhere in the property of the vast estate of their family, and left behind by some long-departed ancestor. Uttaran was looking on amusedly, while listening to his Uncle continue narrating the brief synopsis of the plot. He went on to brief how the production team had come to locate their ancestral home after searching for and scouting numerous options for the most appropriate setting that suited their story and the time period it was set in, the most.

It was then, at that moment that a wonder thought struck Uttaran. What if... what if some ancestor in his family too, had thought of and done the same exact thing? What if someone had indeed decided to hide away some part of the family treasure, some stash of gold or precious stones, in some unknown remote corner of this vast estate. So that in some point in the future, it could be retrieved by himself or by some lucky descendant to whom he would have passed on this little secret. There was certainly a degree of probability. He had read stories about such instances, particularly during the ancient times, when people desperately wanted to hide and protect their hard earned savings from unwanted and prying elements, even from the scheming ones in close relations where trust lay scarce, and secure it for their own heirs and descendants down the line.

It was just a random float of a thought on impulse, but strangely, though not actively, the idea stayed rooted somewhere subliminally at the back of his mind.

It once again came to the fore when Uttaran, now gainfully employed and working for a few years now, had the dual luxury of both time and resources to leisurely follow up on his idea. He decided to regularly visit his native home where his parents now resided, almost every other month and try to dig up whatever information he could about the Grand Patriarch, how he came up with the idea of the ancestral manor home, the internal family disputes and every other thing related to it.

In the preceding few months, Uttaran himself had been trying to dig up as much information and been visiting his maternal relatives, specifically those who had a detailed knowledge of the branched lineages and their respective descendants of the family tree. It had been a very long and tedious undertaking but nevertheless, he had kept on with it. But not much had come out of it.

And one such leisurely discussion on a lazy afternoon with Uncle and the parents had revealed how Uncle had inadvertently stumbled upon the knowledge about the presence of the Grand Patriarch's paternal home, and also about his fruitful visit. Keen and determined to source and research any information that he could lay his hands on, he had also persuaded his sister Suma, to tag along on one of such trips, to a remote village a few kilometres away from their native home, which supposedly had a very old-style manor home somewhere in the deep interiors which was rumoured to be the home of birth of the revered Grand Patriarch.

Unfortunately, Ratna Uncle could not accompany them this time though he had desperately wanted to visit the place again. But he had given the siblings clear and accurate directions to reach the secluded mansion and they were able to locate the house without much trouble.

CHAPTER FOUR

THE PATRIARCHS' HOME

Though it appeared expansive and wide spanned in the exteriors, it did not seem imposing. Probably because it was a single storey structure. The home was surely old, but certainly not dilapidated. It was well-maintained and tidy in the exteriors. The open courtyard in the front was plain empty, save for a sole Tulsi plant in a stone slab that was grouted to the ground. It was hedged by a row of short shrubs on two sides. A short flight of steps at the centre led to the wide, shaded verandah which doubled as an outdoor sit out. It had few old wooden chairs and a teapoy. Uttaran knocked on the door as he looked around. Suma was admiring the row of beautiful plants potted and hanging low from the wooden beams in the ceiling, placed in metal loops with long rods that were hooked on to the beams. An elderly old man came out to enquire at their knock, and though surprised, he cheerfully greeted the young strangers and welcomed them in. He had the siblings seated comfortably and curiously enquired about their intent of arrival. While giving reference to the earlier visit by their Uncle, and upon stating their identities and the name of their ancestral home (which was still a big thing and a matter of awe for the locals in the villages and towns nearby), the kindly gentleman took no time to answer their queries. He asked his wife, an aged lady but not too frail, to make some tea for the unexpected guests, and with utmost patience, shared the most detailed information about the Grand Patriarch.

The elderly couple obviously did not have too many visitors calling in, and the surprise visit by the siblings and their revelation of a distant connection with the Patriarch seemed to further enhance this pleasant respite for them. By the time the initial small talks were done, the tea had arrived.

'So, what would you like to know?' the old man started, as he took a sip from his cup of tea, head bent slightly down to make it easy for him to look at Uttaran from above the top edge of his glasses.

'I am very curious to know about the early life of the Patriarch. We know so very little about him. His parents, for instance?' There were a hundred querying thoughts hurdling all at once in his mind. Suma looked on curiously. 'What was the reason for him to leave his home..this house..and decide to establish settlement elsewhere?' He paused for a second, then sighed 'Sir, there are so many questions arising in my mind, and I do not know whether it is right of me to ask so many questions..and to enquire about, maybe very personal and delicate matters perhaps?'

The kind old man replied assuringly 'Young Man, all that you query about is a matter long bygone. It has been many decades now, even maybe close to a hundred years back, and any discussions regarding those long gone days is only a matter of interesting deliberation now. About why those people, our ancestors, did what they had to do. We can never uncover the exact and precise causes and reasons for such decisions taken, we can only theorise the probabilities. Isn't that right?' He looked at Suma for an approval, and she obligingly nodded with a smile.

'Yes, this was the birth place of the Patriarch, his paternal home. This was home to a joint family then, with a few close families living together, as was the norm then. It still is even now, in some families. The house may not seem too big but it had a large estate of paddy fields and plantations, enough to sustain the entire household. This was how it generally worked in the olden days.'

He paused for a moment, and then continued 'Unfortunately, the Patriarch lost both his parents at a very young age, due to some incurable disease they both may have contracted. It must have been very tough for the young boy. He and his younger sister were the youngest of all cousins, and it is said that they were well taken care of by their uncles and aunts. But as they grew older, the prospect of having to divide the ever-shrinking estate into yet another couple of shares seemed a most unwanted proposition. Especially when the prospective shareholders were two young siblings who knew nothing of the ways of the world. They could be easily shooed away.'

And so the story went. Concocting stories and false rumours regarding the character of the still youthful Patriarch, he was justifiably disowned for causing irreparable disrepute to the family and ordered to leave the family home permanently. The sister, the family decided for some reason, would continue to stay. They would take care of her like their own child. She would not be much of a problem if they held their domination over her.

The young man, innocent and oblivious to the corrosive nature of the recent events, and with no one to support him, had to finally give in and left reluctantly with a heavy heart. Clueless at first, he had not the slightest inkling about what to do then. But given his innate zeal, he decided to leave his village of birth to try and make his fortunes elsewhere. No one ever knew where he went, and how he survived, and how he had struggled. There was no news about him after that. The fact was, no one in his family was even sincerely bothered. On the contrary, deep within, they were happily relieved that he had completed vanished from their lives.

He had never returned to claim his rights to the property by birth and had worked relentlessly to build up a self-acquired and independent worth all his own. The reason could have simply been because, just like it was in every household, the residing home was generally a combined property, owned jointly by various siblings and housed all of them together with their respective families. Some families managed to get along and gelled just fine, but most such homes did have their in-house troubles and squabbling clashes. Understandably.

While the elderly was reciting stories about the Patriarch, Suma interrupted gently and asked for permission to look at the various portraits hanging on the old walls of the living room, which was happily granted.

'A few years later' the old man continued 'rumours came floating about our Patriarch. He had very quickly grown popular in local circles and had aligned himself closely with the powerful Feudal Lords of the times, and had soon come to lord over a very large and expansive estate and had amassed a humongous fortune, something unheard of, in a very short period of time.'

Over a cup of tea and some crispy savouries, the gentleman, now joined by his wife, went on about the Patriarch and his parents. While the lady walked over to give company to Suma, who was now curiously querying about the people in the portraits and in some of the family pictures, the elderly gent made a startling revelation. The Patriarch, even when he had no interest to claim what was rightfully his from the property of his birth place, had on the contrary, after having supposedly amassed a huge heap of a fortune, specially visited his paternal home to graciously hand over a handsome load of gold and other precious jewellery to the family, especially so that the girls of the house would never be in want during their times of marriage, and also to secure a happy subsistence for their post-matrimonial times. He also took his beloved younger sister, widowed and who had a daughter by then, along with him, never to return again.

Meanwhile, Suma had been on a brief exploration inside and around the house accompanied by the old lady while seeking information of the current resident family. She had come out to the front of the home just as the old gent was done with the story of the Patriarch.

After thanking the old couple for their kindness and their valuable time, and also promising to visit them again soon sometime, Uttaran and Suma finally bid them goodbye and left for home.

This trip of the siblings meant a lot to Uttaran. His theory of the Patriarch probably amassing a humongous fortune in a very short span of time was slowly finding solid ground and footing. If he had the largesse to kindly donate such a large portion of goodies to his ancestral home that had treated him so very unfairly in his younger days, then he would definitely have left behind a very generous stash for his very own family and kin. So, the only puzzle part that remained was – whether the Patriarch did actually hide a part of his fortune, and whether anyone in the family had been privy to this information. Or, was there a possibility of some message or cryptic clue left behind in a very subtle or cheeky manner that was to be found by some lucky descendant, or any other treasure seeker, for that matter.

CHAPTER FIVE

A LITTLE ABOUT THE MANOR HOUSE

The native ancestral home, located in the deep interiors of the village, was indeed a very old one. Presumably conceived and initiated around the 1880's, the project, developed in a phase by phase manner due to its vast and expansive layout, would go on to take another five long years before it was entirely completed. It was designed to serve as the mainstay residence of the Village Landlord who had most likely been assigned and authorised for governance and revenue collection in this part of the estate out of several, all of which probably came under a rear Vassal. As was the case in those times before independence, when Kings ruled over the Princely estates and had to overlook administration of their respective kingdoms by appointing nobles and great vassals to govern the far-flung expanses of their very large provinces.

The mansion was built in distinct south-Indian architectural style. The wide-span country house had a flight of steps leading up to the Main Door, a giant of an imposing doorway which was made of hard, solid brown timber wood, with elaborate motif carvings engraved on the thick, vertical side frames. The Main door, which would always remain open, be it day or night, led to a very short walkway which cut both right and left from the doorway, and which themselves, after a few steps of walk, cut inwards at right angles to form a squared walkway that was covered, around the open central courtyard that was around three feet lower to the walkway. There were four sets of a short flight of steps, one for every corridor that led down from it to the central courtyard. There were wooden square pillars, about a foot wide, evenly spaced and standing strong on all the corridors, with each pillar having simple but elegant carvings. The pillars were supports for the ceiling that housed the rooms on the upper storeys of the mansion. The spacious square courtyard in the centre was open to the sky and had nothing but a sole Tulsi Plant housed in a traditional bricked slab, a ubiquitous presence in every household. One had to pass by the main hall adjacent to the primary walkway corridor and then, finally turn left at the end to enter the sit-out (living room) of the home. This was, in essence, the fourth corridor which had been converted to the sit-out or living room. The roof of the country home was covered with Orange-red Mangaluru tiles, now old and withered but still sturdy, with spots of soft green fungi growth distinctly visible. The house exterior architecture was featured and layout landscaped in such a beautiful pattern so as to give an overall impression and feel of an ancient Temple. From the back end of the mansion, a covered shed extended straight out as a long arm in the direction right of the mansion about 70 feet long, and finally cut again downwards to form a long horizontal L. This extension wing, housing a narrow walkway about eight feet wide, had a couple of huge grinding stones and some farmland implements, and was also used as storage to house the rice produce and areca nuts and coconuts from the plantations, and keep them protected from the torrential downpours that were the norm in this part of south India during the monsoons.

The Mansion had six huge bedrooms, three on the ground storey and the remaining three on the upper storey. The lower storey had still further rooms- The Puja or Prayer room, a room for storing the food stock, rice, vegetables fresh and dry, baskets of fruits, pickle containers and some vegetables even hanging down from thin wooden beams on the ceiling, strung by short, flat ropes that had been tightly weaved from dried husks, a big and spacious mother kitchen, with a smaller kitchen adjacently located. A modestly sized dining room could accommodate most of the family members in a single sitting. Just beyond the smaller kitchen was a storage room for holding the kitchen and cooking utilities. The bathrooms, three in number, were all located on the lower storey, behind the Utility space housing a couple of washing machines. The upper storey, apart from the three bedrooms, had a study room, and separate rooms for storage of the paddy harvests. The long attics under the sloping roof also doubled as emergency storage spaces in times of humongous surplus, and their roof tiles just above were placed and secured tight in such a close-knit manner so as to not let any seepage of water in. This was essential because the crop produce had to be kept protected and maintained dry from the heavy downpours which hit the regions unfailingly by the second week of June.

The back portion of the mansion had open spaces where the produce could be laid out in the open, during the dry post-monsoon seasons. There were a couple of cowsheds too, and a small backyard kitchen garden with a few plants that required bare and minimum oversee, and whose border was hedged by colourful and decorative short plants standing close to the intermittent shrubs planted alongside. A couple of banana plantains, and a couple of low green chilli plants, a lone lemon tree and a few creepers of pepper climbing up a short Guava tree completed the green show of the garden.

The mansion was truly expansive, and in order to keep it prim and pristine, the house had three permanent workers, all middle-aged ladies who lived close by, a couple of hundred metres away from the mansion, in their hutments located in the premises of the estate. Most of the workers had their hutments in one corner of the estate, while a few others had built them near the foot of the hillock by which the main approach road passed. While their respective spouses would work in the fields along with the other hordes of workers, the ladies would come to the mansion early morning, and stay the whole course through evening, managing the daily cleaning and kitchen chores and taking care of the cows and poultry, and return to their homes around 7 PM in the evening.

The elders in the family saw to it that the workers were always addressed and treated with respect, and never spoken down to with any signs of asperity. It was a valuable lesson for the younger ones in the family too, that the workers were not their servants who were there to cater to their moods and whims. They were an important part of the family who served a huge helping hand in the upkeep of the home. Many of the cousins had grown up playing around with these very workers and everyone had a special attachment with them. In fact, a very young Uttaran's introductory tryst with the curious betel nut rolled up in a paan leaf happened through one of the lady workers, who would be seen rolling up a paan in a jiffy the moment she got to steal a bit of free time from the various chores.

The main cooking part, though undertaken by the workers, was clearly directed and monitored by the ladies of the house, presently presided over by Uttaran's Mother, looking into even the most minute yet essential part, of culinary details and making sure that the most delectable dishes be served at the table every single time.

The house was now over a hundred and forty years old, almost as if a heritage marvel.

How the Grand Patriarch got hold of such an expansive and boundless mass of land estate had always been an interesting point of debate and discussion amongst the elders of the family. Almost everyone had heard and knew, though very vaguely, about the backdrop and story of the Patriarch, and most elders still vouched that he may have got it as inheritance, more likely as a matter of closure to keep him quiet, as densely forested land banks abounded in plenty during those times and were considered of not much value, and most of the portions were thought to be non-productive while hilly tracts were considered non-arable and utterly useless. While some others figured and were adamantly opinionated that he may have been some sort of a sub-Landlord who had been allocated a large block of estate that he would manage and be responsible for, under some fiefdom of a higher Landlord, who himself may have been under service to one of many vassals under some High Feudal Lord.

Whatever the circumstances under which he came to own such a vast estate, it was very clear that he was extremely prudent and enterprising enough to cash in on the available resources, and wisely put to use his astute acumen to reap maximum dividends. At the least, he had under him around two hundred and fifty acres of land, not located all together in one vast stretch of spread, but scattered away in tracts and spread wide sporadically over a few villages in the vicinity.

And out of this vast expanse, he had selected an enormous tract of around 70 acres in total, all located within a span of around 6 square kilometres. He started out on this mammoth undertaking that was nothing short of a mission, developing an estate that was holding within itself a very vast and expansive outreach of rich plain cultivable lands with agricultural produce, mainly rice, in the water-filled lush green paddy fields, as well as dense forested areas with a variety of flora growing wild and uncontrolled, and a handful of lively brooks rippling through some parts of the green forests.

The far-sighted entrepreneur that he may have been, he prudently decided to flatten out and clear vast portions of the unproductive heaths in the estate handed to him, located strategically close to a flowing stream, with the help of the peasants and local workforce that came under his patronage. The plan had been to put the heaths to productive use by converting them to water-filled paddy fields. This made a lot of sense as monsoons were torrential in these parts and there would be no dearth of water which was very much essential for rice growing activities. The water requirement for the rest of the year would be fulfilled by the flowing stream adjacent to the land tracts, which would stay abundant and brimming due to the onslaught of the heavy monsoons, and could be diverted in parts to local small-hold reservoirs.

The other plan was to fill the vast plain land parcels with arecanut and coconut plantations that would ensure and supplement the income for management of the vast estates that he was to govern.

The Mansion mission was simultaneously undertaken alongside while the other two plans were implemented. This was the regular story that had been passed down the generations pertaining to the creation of what was truly considered a marvel now.

And as it happened with all families, with time, it was only natural that the property of the Patriarch would be divided and shared amongst his progeny. And rightfully so it happened. His children inherited all that was his, but in proportions and in accordance with the matrilineal rule of inheritance. And the Patriarch had only sons, and no daughters. And keeping in accord with the set custom and practice, the Patriarch had to name his one and only beloved sister as beneficiary and equal shareholder to his total immovable properties, with sole proprietary rights to the Mansion. The five sons would have right to stay in the house till the time they were around, but after them, their children would have no legal rights and claims to the house. It seemed unfair, but that was the way the customs of inheritance had always been down south, big family or small, rich family or not. And most such customs, which inherently favoured the female gender, were strictly practised and followed. The more primary reason for this decision was that his sister had been widowed at an early age, and she had a single young daughter to take care of, all by herself.

Till the time the Grand Patriarch was alive, everyone around took care not to hurt his sentiments and consented to all his whims and wishes, but after his demise, skirmishes slowly began to crop up and there was clear friction creeping and evident amongst the various fragmented constituents of the house. The once inseparable Brothers, all of them married by now, and their respective spouses, were routinely into quibbles and clearly displayed their apprehensions, especially towards the one and only daughter of their paternal aunt (the niece of the Grand Patriarch). After their paternal aunt, the mansion would be passed on to this lucky cousin of the five brothers.

The remaining such immovable properties here, such as the cultivation lands and the plantation holding estates, also had been allotted to her.

It was not that the Patriarch had completely ignored and neglected his sons. He had always cared for them. Along with substantial monetary inheritance, the sons had also been allotted large, but lesser-developed land estates in the plains elsewhere, a few kilometres away from this interior village and closer to the main town, where they could further develop their respective properties as they deemed fit. They were, in fact, quite satisfied with the clear demarcation of inheritances but deep somewhere, having to leave and let go of this marvel of a grand mansion pinched hard.

The story goes that till the time the numerous families lived in the mansion, most clashes stayed limited to the verbal, but at times, they had taken very violent turns. Though the violence never ended up in any fatalities, it did make sure that the animosity and vindictiveness in the relations stayed very much alive and stinging, even long after the brothers and their respective families went their separate ways.

Another major disputed aspect of the inheritance pertained to the higher proportion of gold and jewellery ornaments that the sister had been gifted by the Patriarch. Till the time the Patriarch had been alive, the daughters-in-law had been reluctant and mute spectators to this act. But once he had been gone, their non-consent towards such a seemingly unjustified gesture manifested explicitly through their stinging remarks directed intermittently at their paternal aunt and her daughter, supplemented by demeaning ill-treatment of the helpless duo.

And so it followed that whenever one part of the now-fragmented family had to reluctantly move out from the mansion, it was invariably followed by disturbing rumours that a large part of the valuable home jewellery had gone missing from the house. It was just a manner of insinuating not very subtly that the departing family had taken along with them a lot more quantity of the precious movables than what had actually been due to them, as per the demarcation of inheritance, either by fight and force, or by an act of veiled discretion.

And this went on till the time when the last of the brothers finally moved out, leaving the entire palatial mansion to the aunt and her daughter.

The aunt soon got her daughter married, and very sensibly requested and convinced her son-in-law to stay back in the mansion to look after and manage the estate, which her daughter could not have possibly managed had she relocated to her husband's place. The son-in-law, being wise, clearly realised that leaving such a vast estate neglected could result in unwanted elements creeping in and discreetly usurping and claiming ownership of the property, especially when he was in the knowledge of the recent events that had taken place in the family before his marriage.

He took over the reins and with some initial guidance from his mother-in-law and some older experienced workers employed to look over the estate, developed the property further, combining wisdom with patient prudence.

And so it went on, that the property inherited thus, kept on being divided and sub-divided as the new generations followed until finally, out of the large estate, Uttaran's Grandmother, who was fourth in line, and with no siblings, inherited by right and destiny, the whole mansion along with a vast tract of plantations, enclosing within it heaths of rice paddy fields.

Her cousins got the external portions and outhouses of the mansion, which held the extended arms of the mansion, which were primarily storage barns, and the open spaces which were used for drying the various crop produce like rice, coconuts and arecanuts and cashews. The inheritors were free to use their portions as they deemed fit, and one family built a house for themselves right next to the bigger open yard adjacent to the mansion, by extending one end of the storage barn in parallel to the mansion and renovating it to serve as a lengthy hall, which itself jutted both left and right into bedrooms while serving as a long corridor, and finally terminating at the dining room with a big, square kitchen at its very end.

While towards the end of it all, the distribution of the immovable properties were amicably resolved and clearly put to paper, the down-flow of the family jewellery as inheritance had almost reduced to a trickle.

This was precisely what had perked Uttaran's interest.

Out of intrigue, Uttaran, time and again, during his regular visits, would often enquire about this with his mother. He was curious about how the grand Patriarch, who had always seemed to be so very far-sighted and anticipatory in all matters, could not have been prudent enough to make doubly sure that he, and his descendants down the line, would never have to be in want for any needs whatsoever. He had, of course, very thoughtfully created and developed an estate that would, in a way, be perpetually self-fulfilling, with most of the lands being converted to its most productive and beneficial use in the most self-sustaining manner. But to imagine that he would not have contemplated about the monetary and jewellery holdings and also planning their safeguarding, while further ensuring that it be passed on rightfully down the generations, seemed a bit baffling.

Though his mother had mentioned that the mansion was known to hold a lot of jewellery in the olden times, she was not sure about how the movables got divided, and in what quantum, to the various inheriting fragments of the family. She was always given to believe that most of the gold and jewellery disappeared mysteriously when some resenting and aggrieved kin of the extended family would have to leave the house and settle elsewhere as designated.

Many a prosperous inheritance had been lost and withered to rubbles due to incessant and ugly infightings, and the Grand Patriarch would have most likely witnessed such events through his worldly experiences (not necessarily first hand) in his lifetime and having foreseen the same, would have somehow devised a solution to counter the same.

There was a curious theory that was taking shape in Uttaran's mind. If there had indeed been some holdings of precious movables, which undoubtedly would have been the case given the times and the prosperity of the Grand Patriarch, and if most of them seemed to mysteriously disappear with time without any feasible explanation and corroboration pertaining to its whereabouts (he had also made a very large and generous give-away to his paternal family), could it be possible the Grand Patriarch, anticipating such disturbing events in the wake of his demise, may have planned by providence, to hide away a major portion of the precious jewellery and gold in some unknown location, so that it may come handy during some unforeseen turbulent and unfortunate times that may befall on the family in the ever unpredictable future. One never knew what turn destiny could take, but a prudent individual could always anticipate and draw up a planned effort to be prepared beforehand to take the hard and pummelling punches that fate landed, and stay strong and resilient long enough to be able to get back on one's feet and recover.

CHAPTER SIX

THE COLLEGE TOWN

The next morning, Suma had to log in to work and she would be busy the whole day. The parents had to attend a wedding in the town and Uncle had decided to go along with them. Uttaran was not sure about his plans for the day but he did not want to stay back home. He had been racking his brains enough and it was getting to him. Everywhere he looked and every moment he was alone, the picture and story of a treasure sprang up in his head. He needed to get out for a while and get a change of scene.

He had not been to his college for a very long time and this was a perfect opportunity. He had wanted to visit but never got the time for some reason or the other. He had heard from his college friends that the college campus and premises had been improved and developed a lot since the time he had passed out of college. And it had been about five years now. Yes, he would make a visit to his college, and maybe even get to meet some lecturers from his time. He got ready and informed his parents that he would be back by late evening. He took his father's car as the parents had booked a cab for the entire day to visit the marriage venue, and for the further itinerary scheduled.

Uttaran reached his college after a 40 minute drive passing by some scenic villages through the interiors.

The colleges mostly, were set up in the midst and serenity of low hills and expansive greens in the interiors of villages that somehow, though secluded, seemed to perfectly contribute to an environment conducive to pursuing academics. The commercial aspect for this trend was that land parcels came cheap in the interiors and the various enterprises and entities could set up expansive premises for the educational institutions they planned to set up presently, and in the near future.

Uttaran drove his car inside, passing the security at the Main gate and into the parking area in the premises. He smiled as he got down from the car and took a glimpse all around. The college had indeed undergone a complete changeover. The façade of the main building, one among many in the vast premises, was unrecognisable now. Back then, it was just a simple and unassuming plain grey multi-storied building. And now, it had been red-bricked in the entire front, giving it a total contrast to the grey-stone front of the other buildings behind and alongside it. The massive logo of the enterprise that ran the institution hung on the façade in the centre of the building, all chrome and shiny. Students were walking past in and out of the buildings along paved pathways surrounded by green lawns. The institution was minting a fortune, and it showed in the beautiful and lavishly landscaped outdoors, none of which existed during his time in college.

Both Uttaran and Suma had applied for, and secured admission, in different engineering colleges but in the same town, completed their respective courses and graduated just a couple of years apart, both securing a job through their respective campus placements undertaken by the colleges every year before the final graduation of the academic year . The abrupt change from the hurried dash of the city-life to a slow-and-mellow routine at a college located in the deep interiors may have seemed unsettling to many of the city youngsters that took up admission here, but not for Uttaran.

He took a stroll around leisurely, in no particular direction as his memories of the college life all came back in flashes.

Uttaran had, initially, been allotted a room in the hostel located within the premises of the college campus. It was a most monotonous routine that he followed. Morning time, after a quick breakfast in the hostel mess, Uttaran would walk over to the college building which was a 5 minute walk, passing through the huge football and cricket grounds. He would again return the same way for lunch at the mess, head back to college, and return late afternoon after college to have a cup of tea in the hostel mess, and then head back to his room which he shared with another classmate. He hardly ventured out from his room and would come out only for dinner. The only distraction in his room was the window from where he could view the greens around the campus. The students were not allowed to exit the campus during the weekdays, and visits outside the campus were limited within strictly timed deadlines on the weekends. Predictably, the stifling monotony got to him and within a span of a few weeks, he finally applied for stay in another hostel that was affiliated to the college, but was located in the nearest town. Fortunately for him, there were plenty of rooms available as not many students preferred to stay outside the campus premises, and Uttaran got one easily. He had to share the room with two others but that was not a bother. He could finally move about whenever he wanted, without any time restraints.

Once Uttaran was done scanning the college premises and its latest improvements, and meeting up with a couple of his old-time lecturers, he decided to visit his old hostel town, just a 15 minute drive from his college.

The approach road to the town which housed the hostel had not changed one bit in all these years. There was the huge pond that housed a small temple at its centre, accessible by a narrow but sturdy wooden bridge that stretched from the bank of the pond to the temple entrance. Very few, if any, ever visited the temple then and it was the same even now. Hardly a soul could be seen at the place that was more of a swamp now, filled with slush and broad green leaves on the top, and water lilies. The temple had looked dilapidated then, and now, from this distance, it seemed that it could crumble any minute. It could have been a local attraction had the corporation made an effort to clean up the pond and maintain it sparkling and clean. Still, a temple in the vicinity was never neglected, however old and forlorn it may have been. And elders of the town made sure that the temple premises were cleaned and florally decorated and brightly lit up at least once on the special and annual occasion of the town fair that coincided with the first harvest at the end of the monsoons.

The town had a single arterial main road that was single lane, though sufficiently wide, which passed by a few petty shops and restaurants and finally led to the main bus terminal of the town, from where three roads diverged in different directions leading in to the interiors of the little town. Nothing much had changed here either. Except, for the slight increase in traffic congestion.

During his college days, Uttaran had the liberty and time to explore the little town whenever he fancied, and after college hours, this was what he routinely did every day.

He would get down at the bus stop, and instead of heading to his room, he would head in any direction that suited his whims at that moment, and walked down one of the roads that diverged from the bus terminal at the front and back, filled with shops of all kinds and bustling with rush and activity with vehicles jamming the narrow road, and then, gradually simmering down to a deserted stretch just a couple of kilometres down, and which would finally lead to the boundaries of the town and finally lead on to another little village.

For the city-bred, the town would have been a nagging bore. But for Uttaran, the soothing sights of the sleepy town and the villages nearby were a delight. He would yearn for such pleasures. On weekends, when the college would be closed for students, he would wake up early, visit the temple nearby and then walk to one of the many little restaurants at the bus terminal and have a cup of tea, happily gazing and taking in the morning sights at the terminal.

The restaurants would open early to cater to the morning crowds, and along with the restaurants, a couple of newspaper stalls and a row of flower shops right outside the temple would always be in wait for the early morning visitors. After tea, Uttaran would walk down a road with no plan in particular, simply observing the simple old village houses built a little away from the roadside and passing by little petty shops along the way. It seemed like almost everyone in the town, housing no more than 15000 in population then, knew each other and people would be jovially greeting each other every time they passed by.

There were no special tourist attractions as such in the town and the villages in the vicinity, but for those few city-breds that had never seen or experienced what a typical self-sustaining Indian village or town was like, the Town was a very unique attraction.

Uttaran parked his car just outside the bus terminal. He got down, looked around and saw a restaurant that seemed familiar. The name was the same as earlier, but the name display board and the font and design was completely changed. Even the exterior was renovated and showed an attractive front. It had been his favourite haunt on weekend mornings. He entered the restaurant and looked around. The layout had changed, the old worn-out tables and chairs had been replaced with clean new sunmica-top tables and swanky seating benches. The place was full, but not crowded. The waiters were busy taking and serving orders. The space seemed organised, unlike earlier, when the presence of even a few customers at the restaurant gave an appearance of a hurried rush and disarray. Uttaran found a seat in the corner adjacent to a window and waited to order a cup of tea while absolutely enjoying the mad cacophony both outside and inside the restaurant.

He had never known how much he had missed all this. It had been a refreshing and lightening break, this college visit. His mind was feeling light and free. He was ready and raring to go back home and continue with his search for the treasure. Somehow, deep inside, he knew he would find it this time. If he did find it, then he could finally relocate to his native town and live the dream life he had always yearned for.

Life in the city had begun to feel pestering now. The visit to the old college town had just reaffirmed his true and innate desires.

CHAPTER SEVEN

THE LIFE IN DELHI

For the past couple of years, Uttaran had been following a monotonous office routine, and nothing particularly remarkable was holding his interest. Aged 27 now, and almost five years into a job as an IT Engineer in a reputable software services firm in Gurgaon, a bustling city bordering Delhi, the initial elation of a high paying job right after college and smugly getting to work in one amongst the numerous high edifices that made up the city skyline, had gradually subsided.

Uttaran had been having a lot of free time on his hands, and dreary boredom was consuming most of it. There were no familial relatives and cousins residing in the north, and even though he had plenty of acquaintances both in the office and in his apartment society, he had begun to miss home very badly. He had this endless desire to relocate to the south, close to his native home. Close to where his family was.

That was when he decided to do something about it.

What he loved doing most at home was, resting on his armchair with a hot mug of steaming tea and speculate and assess about various topics, some of interest and some, most dull and boring. The stimulating exercise came with reading, and when he would come across a topic he could not fully comprehend, he would close the book and try to imagine and analyse, from scratch, about the fundamental basics of the subject. He had come to the conclusion that no matter how boring a subject sounded or felt, once you understood the core of the subject at its roots, and then moved on higher into its finer intricacies and details, all subjects turned out to be interesting. He was more of a Jack-of-all-Trades and Master-of-None. He would jump on to a topic by whim, stay with it for a couple of days, and when he felt that he had understood the focal fundamentals of it, would abruptly move on to another. The collection of books on his book-shelf, a few of them still mint new and untouched, ensured that he had an uninterrupted access to whichever subject that fancied his whim.

Socially, Uttaran was more of a loner and was averse to late evening and weekend parties conveniently termed as Get-togethers, and this particular hobby was a great way to utilise the free time on hand. On the few occasions where he desperately needed to be out in the sun, he would go down to his apartment society garden within the compound premises and meet his friends, some of whom were his office colleagues while some others acquaintances, who lived on the same floor as him. Being around them and quietly listening to their incessant talks, he would silently ponder on about living in the interiors of a quaint little town or village, yearning for a simple alternate life.

Since the past couple of years however, a novel obsession had taken over. It had been lying dormant within all these years, but gradually came to the fore.

Uttaran had incessantly begun to wonder and ponder about the history of the personality who had built the ancient mansion they resided in, the place he called his native home. He had never entertained a single thought about it in his early younger days. It had never struck him as something wondrous. But as he grew older, the enormity of the legacy of the mansion began to dawn on him. It had been right in front of him, but strangely, he had never ever been curious about this marvel. He had never once bothered to enquire about his past ancestors, their lives, their families and their history. He was both shocked and surprised at the magnitude of his own ignorance.

Then onwards, on every occasion that he visited his parents, he tried to dig up information bit by bit to gain more insight about the Grand Patriarch who had built the mansion. As he gradually unearthed some more about the story of the Grand Patriarch and about his enterprise and initiative, and how he went about amassing a great fortune, it effectively led him to pursue a line of thought as to how the Grand Patriarch may have gone about guaranteeing express safety of his hard earned fortune and holdings, and persistently contemplated over the various possibilities. He would have wanted to put it away someplace safe and secure. It would have to be protected not only from prying eyes and curious elements, but also be protected from the unpredictable weather. Torrential downpours would, on some occasions, be followed by unbearable hot months of summer. It would have to be a spot that could be clearly marked and easily accessible, inconspicuous and yet not overly imperceptible, attracting the least amount of unwanted attention. To rack up such a preposterous idea, and then have to implement and execute such a scheme in an estate with at least 60 acres of land spread in directions all around, would have required head-numbing brainstorming, to say the least. It was a very remote possibility, but nevertheless, a plausible one. And if at all it did happen to be true and one did come upon such a fortune, then he would not have to worry about the feasibility of shifting back home and leading the rustic life.

That was when he decided that he would pursue and unravel the mystery further and more resolutely by making frequent visits to the ancestral home.

CHAPTER EIGHT

THE MANOR LOCATION

The ancestral mansion was located in a village about 11 km from the nearest town. A 20 minute breezy drive from the town, passing through green paddy fields, interspersed with looming coconut, arecanut and rubber plantations and hillocks visible in the distant background, brought one to a landmark overhead water tank, where a sharp cut to the right away from the main road took one down a sloping road about a kilometre long. The road was cut into a hillock so that one side of the road showed the soft incline of the hillock crowded with a mix of trees and wild shrubs, while the other side showed a further spread of a canopy of trees down below. It was a mix of Mango, Jamun, Cashew and Tamarind trees along with varieties of timber and shady Banyans. The wild shrubberies covering the floor of the mildly dense forest were thick and green, with some of them sprouting little variants of colourful wild berries of red and deep purple. The road came with a couple of hair-pin bends and then gradually levelled down to a plain, where a handful of thatched hutments showed up on either side of the road. A few enterprising workers in the fields had found the spot convenient enough, and with the permission of the current residents of the mansion, had built their little places of stay just about the foot of the low hillock.

The road continued slightly further where a slip road cut away from the main to lead into an asphalt entry way that was the driveway to the mansion, with the main road curving slightly away and continuing further ahead into the deeper interiors. It would finally end up a few more kilometres down the road to join a main arterial road at the other end that would be in the vicinity of another little town.

The short driveway led to a dead end where the pair of seating Stones stood, and where the road cut sharply at right angles to the right, finally leading to the Main entrance of the mansion.

As it stood now, the Mansion, majestically seated on a high and vast platform, overlooked around 65 acres of cultivated lands spread out in all directions, and which included both rice paddy fields and the plantations which held within them tall arecanut and coconut trees arranged in rows. Creepers, mainly pepper, filled the gaps in the rows in between. A very small portion of the estate was utilised for growing vegetables that sufficiently fulfilled the needs of the mansion. The surplus was handed over to the workers employed in the fields. It was an enchanting abundance of greenery everywhere you looked.

All of this had not come easy and quick, and had taken many long years and decades to come to fruition. It had required a lot of hard effort and sweat and determination by the past generations over a very long period to work up such a wonder, and now, the current generation was enjoying the benefits.

The mud roads had been converted to tar roads, one main leading to the mansion and couple of by roads branching out, leading to the plantations spread out in scattered tracts of lands, so that easy access was available even by vehicles.

A little bridge inside the estate helped to cross over the lively flowing stream and connected both banks, both sides of which had been optimally developed, extending right upto the foot of the surrounding hillocks.

Every paddy field was bordered by a mudded boundary about 9 inches high so as to ensure it stayed water-flooded during cropping as was essential, and just about thick for a single person to amble on while staying balanced, as if on a single narrow plank. The plantations had been densely hedged mainly by thick and high shrubbery on most sides along with banana plantains, and also with barbed wire fencing in some portions of the boundary so as to deter any trespassing by wild boars that often ventured into the estate inadvertently.

The ancestral home was a favourite get-together venue for family reunions every summer vacation. Grandiose in view and by plan, it was also a favourite venue for the occasions of marriages in the extended family, which were marked as per auspicious dates pondered over and decided by the family priest, and which invited the presence of all the families. The gang of cousins eagerly looked forward to completion of their yearly school exams, and letters would be exchanged regarding their respective dates of travel from their residence cities to the native place. Some would be coming in from as far away as Dehradun in the North and Guwahati in the east, and some from Bengaluru and Mumbai. But the majority of the close relatives were located in Mangaluru, a coastal city which was about an hour and a half's drive from the native village, and also in the nearby towns. The dates of travel were never well synchronised amongst the various families, but invariably, at any given period of time, there would be two or three families staying together for a few days and giving company to Grandma, who was then the permanent resident there, with two of her sons also residing with her.

They were Uttaran's maternal uncles, the youngest brothers of Uttaran's mother, unmarried till then, and were the ones who were managing the agricultural and other general affairs of the estate. Both the Uncles had left the place once they had completed their tertiary education and gained employment soon after, with their new jobs demanding a shift to different cities.

The house would be full and vibrant during those forty days of banter, fun and frolic.

Usually, the weather during the visits in April would be moderately warm, and by the time the families would depart around the end of May, the monsoons would be looming round the corner. The setting would be just right for a bunch of restless teens to roam around in the fields and up the hillocks nearby, and occupy themselves with various outdoor activities, such as trekking through and exploring unseen forest paths alongside the sprightly babbling brooks. The endless leisurely activities would be abruptly interrupted by loud, echoing calls for breakfast, lunch and dinner by the ladies of the house.

The reminiscences of those good times were a major pull for the cousins to get together even after they had grown up and gone their separate individual ways. Not all of them were able to make it often, and those who were able to make the annual trip bonded even more closely now. They would all discuss their present-day scenarios, both work-wise and on the personal fronts, and would purposefully chalk out their strategies for the future. While most of the cousins laid down their elaborate plans, it was always the same with Uttaran. He would somehow wind it all down to ending up at his ancestral home, living in the midst of these lively green pastures.

CHAPTER NINE

UNRAVELLING THE MYSTERY SPOT

Morning time, Suma was logged in to her office work. Uttaran was free and he decided to visit town with Uncle as Uncle had to meet some friends. They were back home just in time for lunch with the parents and Suma. Suma decided to take the day off post lunch as her work schedule was light.

Post lunch, discussions and deliberations with hot cups of tea for company charged and enlivened the atmosphere. Uttaran and his parents, and his Uncle, on some occasions, had done this routine many a times through the past year and based on these ground details, he had been able to shortlist a few probable locations as hide-away spots in the vast estate.

It was late afternoon and after a while, both brother and sister headed to the Stones, chatting about their cousins they very much missed.

The seating Stones, as it was named such by all, was a pair of stone slabs, located a few feet distant from each other at right angles, and spanning about five feet wide and four feet from the ground level, and supported on a couple of vertical stone slabs, just perfectly designed to allow seating for four comfortably. Grouted to the ground and shaded by a humongous old Mango tree standing adjacent, they overlooked the main road passing by just a few feet below and alongside, and the vast paddy fields spread out directly in front with the workers going about their daily grind diligently, and the gaze stretching far to the hillocks, distant yet clearly visible. It was a sweet spot for lazing on sunny afternoons with light breeze blowing, invigorated by rustic scenes such as watching the occasional buses pass by intermittently, and having a little chit chat with the familiar locals and querying little nothings with school children walking past. Happenings in the local village and town communities, be it important or inconsequential, all came to the fore through some small talk here. The stones were located about seventy feet from the mansion, and at a dead end which visitors had to pass by, and turn right before you ended up at the Main Entrance of the mansion. One only had to sit there to enjoy a lease of rejuvenation.

Uttaran had not mentioned anything to Suma yet, about prospective hideaway spots for the treasure. He decided to test her inklings about the possibility.

'Tell me Suma. Has it ever occurred to you that there might be a treasure hidden somewhere here?'

'Where..here?' she asked perplexedly. 'By these stones?'

'No, not 'here' here. I meant somewhere in the mansion.' He paused for a moment, then continued. 'You had heard what the old gentleman at the mansion had mentioned. About the Patriarch coming over to hand over jewellery and gold to the family.'

'Yea..so what?' Suma snapped.

'Don't you think that if such substantial wealth was handed over by the Patriarch to his paternal family, he would have amassed a lot, lot more for himself and his close family. I personally feel that he not only passed on substantial riches to his near and dear ones, but he could have also stashed away a major portion secretly. You know, sort of a contingency plan.'

'Why do you think so?' Suma queried inquisitively.

'Because..Every time I discussed about the family's inheritance with Mother, it always turns out that all the riches and precious items just dwindled and finally disappeared down the line. I accept and understand that a major portion would have been passed down and spread across the generations, but it is hard to digest that the mansion does not have even a bit of jewellery and gold left for the current generation of siblings as inheritance.'

Initially, Suma felt that that such a possibility seemed too distantly remote. Firstly, stumbling upon such serendipitous fortune never did happen in the lives of the common people, and secondly, if at all such a treasure had been hidden by the Grand Patriarch, would it not have been chanced upon and found by one of the occupying residents in the past 100 years or so.

Uttaran accepted that the said fact would not have been exactly untrue, but he also pressed on the slight probability that the treasure had not been discovered as yet. He threw a few spots for deliberation over where the treasure could have been tucked away, given the spread of the expansive estate. Such a deliberation would also reveal the possibility of whether the treasure, if it ever existed, could have been already taken by a most lucky beneficiary.

The stones, for instance. The stones were indeed a distinct and prominent landmark, and a perfect spot for locating precious jewellery underneath, all wrapped and bound up tightly in thick cloth and placed in a hard container so as to keep it watertight and immune to any degrading attack from the surrounding soil. It was a location impossible to forget and extremely easy to pin point to, for the exact spot of dig. A departing old patriarch short of breath and words would, if he ever needed to convey the presence of the treasure in the most clear and concise of expressions, just had to fleetingly mention – Just Dig under the stones.

But such landmarks were numerous and scattered all over the estate. And from where would they begin?

Uttaran remembered his father's suggestion that in order to get a hint and gist of the possibilities of hiding spots, you had to put yourself in the shoes of the Patriarch so as to try and get a feel about how he would have strategized and gone about the entire exercise.

The duo began to throw and bounce ideas off each other. Though Suma was initially reluctant, the idea of just theorising and playing with such a scenario in the head was stimulating enough, and she sportingly joined in for the fun of it.

A worker of the house was passing by them, making way towards the mansion, and they kindly asked him to send someone from inside with a flask of hot tea and a couple of tea cups.

'What would you do? If you had a big, big fortune and you had to hide it someplace?' he asked Suma.

She was looking far out at the fields. 'I would seek a spot, far but safe. So that no one could find it easily.'

'Not even your family? Your descendants? For whom the fortune was meant to be passed on onto?' he countered. 'Let's say, given a scenario, that you got old and sick. And immobile. So that you are not able to move about easily. How would you retrieve the riches?

Or maybe, even a part of the riches, if you needed it desperately?'

She turned to look at Uttaran questioningly.

He continued 'Let's assume that you are not able to even speak coherently. Then, how are you going to communicate and convey about the presence of such a fortune hidden away, especially for the family?'

'So then, what according to you is the ideal hiding spot?' she retorted, with a hint of irritated ire.

A couple of bikes whizzed by as the duo continued their assessment. The tea flask had also arrived by then, thankfully. Uttaran poured some tea into the cups and let Suma take a sip. She too, was addicted to tea and any subtle signs of an impending migraine had to be instantly suppressed. The tea would calm her down instantly.

The Patriarch had an array of spoilt choices. He could have hidden it somewhere at the foot of one of the distant hillocks, and cleverly marked the spot by planting a tree over it. Or even with a short stone pillar, that would also mark the border of his property, which would ensure that no one tampered with or uprooted the marker. He could also have hidden the treasure in the rice mill, located adjacent to the stream, and where the raw harvested rice from the paddy fields would be deposited and de-husked. No one would ever guess about such a hideaway.

There were many such landmark hot spots all around. But even if one did hide it in such a spot, which was a little distant away from the main mansion, would it be considered prudent?

What if, for some reason, one became immobile due to disease or old age and could not access the treasure spot himself, and had to communicate and convey the exact position of the hidden treasure to a loved one. Someone, whom the secret had to be passed on to.

Imagining an old dying man on his bed in the mansion desperately pointing his shivering hands out somewhere towards the skies while mumbling incoherently in a state of utter delirium to his dear ones about some treasure he had caringly left for them to enjoy. The outcome did not seem too pleasant.

No. The treasure had to be somewhere close. And near.

Suma was now contemplating over some possible hideaways closer to the mansion. There had to be some options which would be prominent yet subtle, and not too easily conspicuous so as to attract direct attention. The stones they were seated at, definitely fitted the bill. But the more one tinkered deeply with the thought, the more unlikely and remote it seemed. The problem lay in its location.

Just behind both the stones standing perpendicular to each other, and where the mud road ended to curve right to the mansion, the ground dropped steeply about seven feet below, where a channel passed by to supply water to all the tracts of land fields nearby where the rice paddy grew.

The water channel was a single, narrow waterway about a half-a-foot in depth and a foot wide made simply by gently spading through the soft earth along the outer edges of the numerous paddy fields, and water was let in to the paddy field through intermittent openings in the mudded boundary of the channel.

The single channel, diverged from a small man-made water reservoir, was a very narrow waterway and was a crucial conduit for the fields as it snaked through the entire vast estate and also branched out at a couple of points to pass by the many square tracts of fields scattered adjacent to each other. It ensured uninterrupted water supply to keep the paddy fields flooded, an important and critical aspect for rice growing, during the non-monsoon seasons.

This meant that the placement of the stones right above the channel could be compromised, as and when it was deemed in the future that the water channel may have to be re-routed through another direction for even more efficient and purposeful irrigation. This in turn, obviously implied that the stones could be prone to a dig-up phase anytime, and someone could end up with an inadvertent discovery of the treasure.

The tall and beautiful Mango Tree, playing a perfect high green canopy to the stones was also not likely to be chosen, as it was too magnificent to be cut down or uprooted.

After deliberated discussions and crossing out the long list of the probable hiding spots, it all came down to the mansion and its close and surrounding proximity. Somehow, the siblings felt that the spot had to be closer to home. The short length of the walkway from the stones to the main entrance stairway did not appear to have any such distinct spot that would fit the bill. The steps leading up to the main entrance did not seem special either, that suited to fulfil such a purpose. The steps were, on both to the left and right, were planked by what had originally been mudded square-shaped flower beds, and which had now been entirely brick-floored and held only potted plants now.

Once inside the mansion, yes, there were numerous spots where the Patriarch could have easily hidden the treasure. Some so inconspicuous, even a cleverly camouflaged hint or marking would not seem obvious, unless one was specifically looking for the treasure.

That is the way the mind works. One could be present in a room full of objects and not find anything suitable at all, but once you have a definite purpose, like for instance, to search and look for something circular in shape, or for the colour green, you would find all sorts of items circular and green amongst all the garbage popping up at you.

Uttaran and Suma were very clear about what they were looking for, and they were certain if they looked hard enough and kept their minds open to all sorts of possibilities, the potential hideaway spots would just start appearing.

During the course of the past few months preceding his latest visit, the conviction of presence of a hidden treasure had firmly ingrained deep in Uttaran's mind.

The elders were on their late afternoon siesta breaks, and Uttaran and Suma sat down on the couch in the living room overlooking the courtyard and continued skimming with their theories.

Apart from the living room and main bedrooms in the mansion, there were a number of other smaller rooms, some entirely separate while some others were part of the bigger bedrooms on both the lower and upper storeys, planned as a mini store room for each of the master ones. The separate smaller rooms were functioning as storage for the harvested rice and some of the vegetable produce, the areacanuts, and also the coconuts, most of which were dried here and then de-husked before being crushed to source the edible oil used in cooking. It was very unlikely that they could hold a hideaway spot.

After a series of discussions, Suma had gotten exhausted and sleepy and decided to go upstairs to one of the bedrooms and take a short nap. It was a hot afternoon and sleep inducing. Uttaran had moved on to the old wooden armchair with the long extended armrests. It was more of a sleeper and less of a sitting chair, given its long spread of a curved sitting base with a sloping backrest, so that one could lay out their legs on the armrests and enjoy a short siesta, or more probably designed to portray an imposing show of power and authority of the erstwhile landlords, discussing affairs of the estate with the workers who would be standing down in the courtyard, taking instructions with arms folded tightly across their chests, with eyes lowered and humbly bowing.

Uttaran closed his eyes and was deeply contemplating. The entire night before, he had not been able to sleep as he had felt restless. He was not able to clear his mind from the myriad thoughts binded to the treasure. And since breakfast in the morning with his parents and deliberating till late afternoon with his sister, he had been constantly racking his brains. The mental exhaustion had gotten to him and had drained him completely, and he never realised when he fell into a deep slumber.

It was evening when his mother gently prodded him awake. He opened his eyes, glanced around dreamily, and went back to sleep.

CHAPTER TEN

THE VISION

The Patriarch, with full vigour and passion, would have gone about the planning and execution of this grand project. Going through the grind day in and out, he would have finally seen the mansion project through to completion. And then, having all his family members move in, would have happily cherished the company of his near and dear ones. He would have gone about ensuring full providence not only for the entire family, but also for all the generations to come, by developing the vast estate in a manner that would be self-sustaining and of continual and prosperous bounty.

Somewhere down the line, the Patriarch would have noticed subtle lines of division creeping up in the family, and would have charted a plan for clear partition and ownership of the estate during his lifetime. Both movable and immovable.

He also would have come up with a contingency plan, unknown to them. A sort of emergency corpus...just in case. One never knew when the bad times would or could come upon the family. But one could always anticipate, given the good virtues of aged experience and knowledge, and choose to be prudent.

A part of the jewellery ornaments and a just amount of gold, all packed up in a tight little holding, and which could be tucked away in a spot not too obvious, and yet easily marked and from where it could be retrievable.

The Patriarch would have contemplated deep and hard, looked around, and thought long about it. A place not too far-off. A spot somewhere close...that he could access even when he would be old and aging. A spot that he could keep an eye on, always. Even in the worst case of immobility and being bedridden. Someplace...which could always be clearly seen from every corner of the house..someplace...someplace..someplace.

Uttaran woke up abruptly, opened his eyes and looked about.

And there it was.

Right out in the courtyard, lit up by a single diya under the evening sky. The TULSI SLAB.

Uttaran got up from the chair slowly and looked at the slab holding the Tulsi plant. Observing the slab silently, a million thoughts dashed around excitedly in his mind. All of them instantly converged to an image that was a package of bounty which was buried deep under the slab. Uttaran smiled. He had just been struck by a flash of genius.

He heard his mother calling him and the rest to the dining room. Dinner was ready to be served. Uttaran was famished, and he was glad to hear the call and quickly entered the dining room and took his seat. He was anxious to follow up on it the next morning.

CHAPTER ELEVEN

THE TULSI SLAB

The Tulsi brick Slab, about four feet in height and with a square base of around one feet, housed the revered Tulsi plant in a recessed bowl at its top which was an ubiquitous presence in the courtyards and verandahs of most old houses. It was considered to be a giving and benevolent benefactor to the home it resided in, akin to the very reassuring presence an old and elderly beloved in the family. It was not only considered to be auspicious but was also known for its medicinal qualities which helped in promptly bringing down a light cold or a mild sore throat.

In his quest for further information, Uttaran had enquired whether there were any old photograph albums, not of the recent old times, but of the very early times when the Patriarch and his family had just begun to move in and settle in their new manor home. Uttaran's Mother did recollect that there were indeed a few albums tucked away someplace in one of the upper-storeyed bedrooms, which one she was not completely sure. The albums obviously, were not of any interest to the present generation, and would be handy only to those few curious minds which were keen to be acquainted with the bygone ancestors.

There were three bedrooms on the upper storey and Uttaran went through the cupboards and recessed wall cabinets and got out all the albums that were there, and placed them on a bed. The albums were old, but not damaged or frayed, probably because they had never been moved out of their permanent enclosures for a very long time.

Uttaran sat down on the floor and scoured through them, and while going through the family albums of yore, had very many stills arousing great curiosity in him.

Some faintly fading photographs had the earliest family members, most of whom he failed to identify, staring blankly at the then uncommon camera, with the gents seated in the front row and a few children seated cross-legged on the floor frowning, along with a couple of Alsatian dogs amidst. The ladies would be standing behind, with a few children in tow. Some others showed families present in the various spaces, both exteriors and interiors, of the vast mansion. Some stills showed the indoor storages full of jute gunny bags, complete with husks and barns of hay brim to the top while wide open spaces of the mansion would be occupied by spreads of arecanuts laid out to dry under the sun. Some others showed hordes of workers in the fields, bending down to lay the little rice saplings in neat rows in the brown wet blankets of paddy fields.

Uttaran, though intrigued by the identities of the various strangers who were his ancestors, was intently looking for something specific. He had been browsing through the many albums looking for a still of the central courtyard. Finally, he found one. The Tulsi slab was there, in the exact spot where it stood even to the present day. The walkway around the courtyard looked a little different, but that was understandable as a few alterations to the mansion had been known to have been undertaken, as and when stringent property demarcation situations demanded so. Uttaran flipped over a few more slips of the album, looking for some familiar faces in the extended family. Some of the faces in the album showed clear connection to the Grand Patriarch, what with the similarities in the facial features. He flipped some more, and then firmly clapped the album shut. He was just about to move to the next album when he stopped still.

He quickly opened the album again and flipped through it again, this time from the back. He had seen something, yet missed it. He came to the monochrome photograph where the family, with the Grand Patriarch dressed in traditional grand attire, was posing for a still in the central courtyard.

And bang in the centre of the courtyard was the Tulsi. Now, this was odd.

Uttaran went back to another album and flipped through the photo slips, and one of them showed the Tulsi in a corner of the courtyard, its current and present place of standing.

The Tulsi slab had been moved.

As per the original design, it had been grouted to the ground right in the centre of the courtyard, and then, for some reason, had been ungrouted from its spot, and relocated to its current position in the courtyard.

Uttaran was slightly relieved. This was a slight but directive vindication of his theory.

The Tulsi Slab in the mansion being relocated by the family from its original position suggested the possibility, however remote, of an intention to bury and hide something deep under the current landmark. It could have been relocated to accommodate some other structure, but there was no other in the courtyard except for the Tulsi Slab. What better than to have a landmark that was right under one's nose, visible and accessible at all times, and ensuring by its own good virtue that it would always remain protected and untouched. It seemed most credible.

Uttaran went down to the kitchen where his mother was working and showed her the pictures. She was genuinely surprised and was bewildered by this strange aberration. After looking again in detail at both the pictures, she tried to remember any such event or talk about relocating the revered slab in those early times. Strangely, there was nothing. No story at all connected to this mystery.

Uttaran went to wake his sister up. He prodded her gently. Suma woke up, albeit reluctantly, and irritated by this unwanted intrusion. Uttaran asked Suma to follow him downstairs. He held up the album and flipped to the still showing the Tulsi in the centre. He then told Suma to look out into the courtyard. Suma looked back and forth, first the courtyard and then the picture, a couple of times. She finally turned and looked towards Uttaran, astonished.

Uttaran was smiling, looking down at the picture. Could something really be buried down there? Under the Tulsi slab? Though slightly cynical earlier on, Suma nodded and consentingly aligned with the possibility of this incredulous theory.

But how would they go about it? The duo decided to consult with their parents and Uncle.

It was late afternoon tea time, and the family was seated at the dining table, waiting for snacks and some steaming tea. There was the usual banter and chit chat about the relatives and close family friends and what everyone was upto. Finally, it was time and Uttaran brought up the subject to Mother, Father and Uncle. He and Suma discussed the theory that they had hypothesised.

The parents were skeptical at first and were very clear that the theory was too preposterous to be true, but again, the possibility of a treasure hidden somewhere in the mansion seemed a bit vaguely probable to mother, given the past stories she had heard about the mansion's riches and fortunes.

CHAPTER TWELVE

THE EXECUTION

Uttaran and Suma were more concerned about how to go about the digging part under the TULSI. But before undertaking such a mission, they had to be at least partly sure that there was indeed something hidden and buried down under.

While in Delhi, during his tryst with various diversified subjects in the weekends, he had read about how some enterprising people made their living as modern-day treasure hunters. They would read up on a territory, dig up its past historical events and then try to deduce logically and scientifically, whether or not there was a high or remote possibility of the terrain having some ancient treasures or antiques connected to those events buried deep down in its soil belly.

Because they were worth a lot of money, if sold to the right collectors.

Now, before undertaking such digging missions, these entrepreneurs had to take the requisite permission from the relevant authorities, or from the land-owners, as would be the case. And then, finally, they would go about scanning the land terrain with some very hi-tech hand-held equipment such as gold and other precious metal detectors, which would indicate presence of such material deep under the earth by emitting loud and distinct beeps, and in some cases, even forming a distinct image on the scanner display screen. While it did not ensure 100%

accuracy, but hitting gold, literally, 96 times out of 100 definitely drew up a very good performance chart.

Uttaran had looked up similar equipment online on the internet, for general information on how they actually worked, and how authentic and result-oriented it truly was in the real world. He had browsed through real-life stories of entrepreneurs connected with this profession, and while some sounded truly dejected, there were a few stories that had thrown up positive results. The cost of procuring such highly sophisticated equipment was detrimentally high, and spending such a fortune on a mission that one was not truly sure of, seemed a dampener to Uttaran. He would have to make do with a much more economical alternative. But he had to arrange it. Out of sheer curiosity, he had ordered a single gold-detector back in Delhi. When it had arrived, he had excitedly opened the contents of the package and without wasting any moment, had tested it using a few of the gold coins that he had bought as investment from his savings.

The gold coins, even when placed deep under a layer of set of cushions, were quiet satisfactorily detected by the hand-held detector equipment. The detector had also been able to detect other metals as well, and the pointer on the detector marked and identified which category of metal was specifically detected.

Satisfied with the working quality of this sample, he had confidently ordered another set of equipment, more expensive than the previous one but with much more sophisticated features. He had marked clear instructions for delivery directly to the ancestral home.

The gold-detector equipment that Uttaran had procured, had been delivered a few months ago at the ancestral home. The detector equipment was essentially a portable detector with capability to detect presence of metals located at a certain depth underground. It had a circular scanning base about a foot in diameter mounted on a set of small wheels, and the base was attached to a long handle about three feet long so as to allow easy control and manoeuvrability to the equipment handler. Presence of metal underneath would result in beeps emitted by the detector as well as by a pointer movement on a marked gauge.

While the parents had looked on inquisitively, Uttaran had assembled the pieces and checked the working procedure of the equipment the last time he had visited home, and had already tested it by roving it around in the open spaces adjacent to the mansion. The portable equipment was very light and easy to handle and manoeuvre, and had beeped several times through the testing exercise session. This was very normal, and the manual had mentioned it someplace that the detector settings would have to be calibrated as per the exact nature of metal that was to be detected, or else there would be random beeps going off time and again.

The workers had looked on in amusement while Uttaran had gone about the testing routine. After a few rounds of trial and error, the machine came to be calibrated just right after a delicate touch of fine-tuning. He was extremely confident the machine would work fine and would come handy in his treasure endeavour. Once he was completely satisfied with the proficiency and accuracy of the machine, he had it dismantled and segregated the few pieces and packed it away in a safe corner in the bedroom, to be used later on the right occasion.

The time had come now.

He was up early dawn the next day and after a cup of hot tea, he got down right away to business. He assembled the metal detector and put on the earphones, switched the Machine ON and walked over to the TULSI SLAB. The family was still asleep. It was peace and quiet all around. Uttaran wanted to carry out this particular procedure undisturbed and without any distractions.

Uttaran got to the edge of the base of the slab and manoeuvred the detector expertly. He had become used to the machine now. He had experimented with it a few times earlier in the mansion, and he had got quite accustomed to its working and its various indications, some of which being very clear false alarms. He had also used it just for the fun of it in the vicinity of the cowsheds located behind the mansion, where intermittent but strong beeps led to unearthing of a small copper vessel buried just a couple of feet under the soft earth. Though the vessel was completely useless, it boosted Uttaran's confidence in the resourcefulness of the detector. He had not put his money entirely to waste.

There was no signal whatsoever, and Uttaran moved it around the whole square perimeter of the base of the slab. There was still no beep. He looked at the Pointer Gauge and moved the detector again briskly, back and forth. The Pointer moved. There was no beep, but the pointer needle had just jerked to the centre of the analog display. Uttaran moved the detector away from the slab, and the pointer instantly slumped back to its original position. His heart was beating faster now. He slowly moved the detector towards the slab again, and the pointer once again sprang up on the display. Uttaran was flummoxed. He was not sure why the beeper had not gone off. He removed the earphones and replaced them again in his ears. No sounds yet. He checked the volume knob on the detector dash. It was at zero. Shaking his head at his foolish thoughtlessness, he slowly increased the volume, and the beeps came on.

Uttaran was smiling now. His theory was closer to being corroborated. There was definitely something down there, and metal buried down and under a Tulsi Slab could imply only one thing – Hard Fortune. No one would have taken the trouble to hide heavy utensils under the slab, for sure.

Uttaran pulled back the machine away from the slab, switched it off completely and then re-started it. He waited for a few moments to check for any false alarms, and then re-set the parameters of the machine to Gold, and then, once again moved it towards the slab. And there again, The Pointer skipped on the display just as a loud beep started emitting in the earphones. He looked up at the sky and smiled. He took off the earphones and switched off the machine and let it sit on one side of the courtyard, and slowly walked up to the living room. He needed to sit, and take the whole situation in. He crossed his hands behind his head and looked up. He could not believe what had just happened. Could it really be there? He got up excitedly and went to the kitchen to make himself another cup of tea. How great it tasted!

Everyone was still asleep.

By the time he had finished his tea and begun to gather what had just happened, his parents had woken up and saw the machine out in the courtyard. They enquired whether he would have tea before he was about to start the process, and he replied with a smile that he was already done.

He couldn't hold his excitement any longer. He sat both of them down next to him and told them that the detector had definitely and positively signalled a presence of metal under the slab, and now the only thing that remained to be done was to dig under the slab. How it was to be undertaken without damaging the auspicious plant that it held, and also without drawing too much attention, was the perplexing conundrum.

Uncle, who had also woken up by then and had joined the parents, proposed a suggestion.

They would scour the local markets and shop for a Tulsi slab similar in look and design, and then, after finally purchasing a slab closest in all senses to the original slab, take it to a handicrafts craftsman and give the slab an old finishing so that it would match with the old and weathered features of the Tulsi slab. The motive was that if, during the execution of this mission, the Tulsi slab got damaged and was beyond repair, they could immediately replace it with the new one and not leave the spot empty, which otherwise would draw instant attention and queries about what the residents were upto.

The suggestion was approved and accepted by all. After breakfast was done and without wasting further time, the siblings drove their car to town and headed directly to the nurseries on the main road in the outskirts just outside of town. They found one, strikingly similar in shape and height, paid for it and asked the nursery vendor to transport it to the local mart where the many craftsmen of the town were categorically allocated shops at, where they could promote and sell their handicraft wares both to the local gentry as well as the tourists that streamed in occasionally, especially during the peak season in the holiday vacations.

Village tourism had begun to make its mark and the town was beginning to see a flow of curious tourists very eager to savour a pinch of the village life. The handicrafts mart, though already popular in local circles for their artistic and functional hand-made products like the bamboo and cane furniture and decorative wares, had further got an invigorating boost due to this happy influx of tourists they could cater to, along with the few temple and pilgrimage towns in the vicinity.

Uttaran and Suma had no trouble in finding an expert painter in the mart, and they explained to him precisely what they wanted, and that he would be handsomely rewarded if the result was exactly as they desired. The confused artisan, though perplexed with the curious requirement of a bland and weathered finish with a bit of dull-green fungi touching, was more than happy to produce the desired result when he got to know the remuneration he was to gain for his expert efforts.

The siblings left the Slab with the artisan after giving him clear instructions for place of delivery the next day.

Mother meanwhile, had asked the head servant to gather a few workers for the excavating job to be undertaken a couple of days later, so the hard labour part of the job was arranged.

The only concerning matter that troubled them was about the workers that would come in for the digging and uprooting of the slab. The workers, just like any other set, were prone to gossiping and within no time, the word would spread in all directions about the find. This had to be managed somehow with some generous compensation. A regular tip for a round of evening drinks at their favourite country shack would not suffice.

The day finally arrived. One could feel the tense energy in the air. The Tulsi slab had also been delivered the previous evening. The artisan had tried to put his best efforts but even then, one could make out that the slab was devoid of the desired old and weathered look. But they had to make do with whatever they had at hand. The workers had also gathered in the courtyard. Uttaran had asked a couple of them to vigorously rub mud and dust all over the new Tulsi slab to make it appear even more faded.

The rest of the workers picked their digging tools and got to work without wasting any time. The parents and Uncle were seated in the living room now, watching over the progress while Uttaran and Suma stood nearby in the shade, directing and instructing the workers now and then, not exhibiting any of their giddy excitement rumbling within.

The pointed metal bars were hitting the mud furiously and hard, chipping the edges of the slab. The workers were profusely sweating now, making their dark-skinned bodies glint under the morning sun. But they were habituated to such gruelling hard work, as they had been doing so for many years in the paddy fields and plantations all through the various seasons.

It was soon afternoon, and the workers decided to take a break for lunch. They would be served lunch in the mansion kitchen so as to save precious time. They had lunch while merrily making banter, while Uttaran and Suma had a round of tea while discussing the matters at hand. The detector had buzzed and beeped, but even with such sophisticated state of the art, there was always a minuscule dot of a chance for error.

There was a light zephyr pleasantly blowing by, and the workers briskly got down to another gruelling session of excavation. The three workers were furiously digging through from all corners of the slab, while the fourth was spading the soft mud onto a cane basket and dumping it all in a corner of the courtyard. The mud would be required later to refill the dug-out when the new Tulsi slab would be re-grouted.

The slab had begun to come loose from its holding in the mud, and the workers slowly lifted the slab, with the Tulsi plant still staying put inside the bowl shaped recessed space at the top of the slab. They placed the heavy slab very carefully on the ground a little bit away from the dug hole, and then respectfully bowed before it, treating it no less than the other deities they so deeply revered. They began to dig even harder and freely now, with no obstacles remaining to delicately manoeuvre around. After a couple of hours, they had dug about four feet deep into the earth when Uttaran decided to get his detector to work. There was not even the slightest hint of any indication on the detector. According to his initial findings, the buried metal should have been located at a depth not more than four feet into the ground.

They decided to break for tea and the workers sat down adjacent to the dug-out, while Uttaraan and Suma walked over to the parents. Uttaran seemed a little dejected but did not show it openly whereas Suma was very optimistic that they would soon hit the gold spot. The workers had finished their tea and snacks and came back enthusiastic with even more vigour. Uttaran switched on the detector again and hovered the base around the hole. The beeps were barely buzzing now and had sounded weak and feeble. Nevertheless, he instructed the workers to dig on.

A further two feet of digging later, Uttaran got the detector again. This time, he got down on his knees and lowered it into the pit as deep as he could reach, and hovered it around lightly in the air. The beeps had entirely vanished. He glanced at the display. The pointer had not moved even by a single bar, frozen still in its base position. He asked one of the workers inside the pit to hold the detector to the ground and scan it. But the result was the same.

Uttaran was completely flummoxed.

He got up, pulling up the detector and asked the workers to halt work for a while. He took Suma aside to where the dug-out slab had been kept and conversed in a whisper.

'The treasure should have been hit by now. We are at more than six feet now and no beeps at all.'

'There must be a mistake' Said Suma. 'Maybe the settings on the detector need to be calibrated right. Let's reset it and lower it again.'

'But you had noticed the detector had beeped perfectly before we had begun the dig.' Uttaran replied. 'And beeped hard. The pointer had worked perfectly to the same settings. No..something's amiss.' He pondered and despondently concluded 'Maybe it is elsewhere. Maybe we are looking for it in the wrong place.' He walked over to the slab pulling with the detector behind him and looked at it deeply, as if searching for an answer. He turned around slowly to talk to the workers when suddenly, a thought struck him.

He turned back slowly, took a hard look at the slab, and took the detector towards the slab and placed it towards the bottom of the slab. The detector beeped. Uttaran stood still and did not move one bit, and looked back at the detector. The pointer had moved and it was now stuck at the exact marking bar where it had initially pointed, before the dig had been initiated. Uttaran moved it closer to the slab and all around, and the beeps got louder. It was now a continuous buzzing beep, not ready to stop. He moved the detector away from the slab and the beeping got fainter and finally stopped. Uttaran placed the detector on the bottom of the slab again, and the beeping re-started loud and clear. The pointer did not move at all now, firmly fixed on the bar and stubbornly still at the gold mark. Uttaran laid the detector down and got down on his knees and bent low to closely inspect the base of the slab. He tapped the edges at the bottom and asked Suma to take a look.

They looked at each other, and Uttaran finally said 'Maybe it is in here, inside the slab. At the bottom.'

'Is it possible?'

'Yes. Why not? This is indeed a perfect spot for hiding. Safe from the soil and weather, and total assurance that it would not be discovered even by chance. No one would ever unnecessarily go about breaking up the slab for some trivial reason. Don't you think so?'

Suma nodded in agreement, albeit still quite unsure.

Uttaran and Suma walked over to the parents and Uncle, still seated in the living room. They had been watching the entire proceedings from a distance quietly. The duo updated about the findings and their plan to break open the slab. The parents approved with a slight hint of alarm. After all, they were going to break the holding slab of their beloved Tulsi.

Uttaran asked the workers to come out from the dug-out, and directed them to carefully pull out the plant, with the entire mud and soil base that the plant was firmly rooted to, and place it carefully in a wide cane basket. After it was done, he instructed them to break open the solid bottom of the slab. The workers promptly pulled the slab down so that it lay horizontally on the ground, and once again bowing to it, started hammering the bottom from all sides. The bottom started to give way and chunks of brick and stone fell off, crumbling. The workers were hard at it when suddenly, there was a mild clang. One of the blows had hit solid metal. Uttaran abruptly stopped the workers and looked down among the crumbles.

He bent down to look clearly, and he finally saw it.

Covered in reddish brown dust from the crumbled and powdered bricks, he slowly picked up the square shaped container and wiped off the dust lightly with his hands. It was wrapped in cloth, but he could very lightly see the ornamental engravings on the cover of the container. It felt heavy. He turned around to look up at Suma, smiled at her and handed over the container. Suma was gleaming, and she looked at her parents and slowly held the container up high in her hands. The parents were smiling. They called her over to the living room while Uttaran directed the workers to go have some tea and snacks, after instructing them to collect all the rubble and neatly pile them in a corner of the courtyard. And then, once it was done, he told them to re-fill the spot of the slab with the earth that had been dug out, and then have the new Tulsi Slab grouted into the original spot.

Suma had handed over the container to mother. They all went inside to one of the bedrooms to check the find. It was wrapped in a thick cotton cloth. She untied the knots and inside was a shiny silver box, square shaped and a small vertical latch that held the hinged top cover shut tight on its base. They took it to the God's Puja room and placed it at the foot of the deities, and bowed respectfully with their hands clasped together. And then, with a prayer in their hearts, they slowly opened the top up.

The contents inside made their eyes gleam with joy.

There were precious ornaments shimmering on top, and below which were laid out a couple of rows of shiny gold coins. Mother scooped both her hands inside the container to pull up the contents further. The moment was ecstatic as the ornaments slided down from her fingers back into the container. Father overturned the container and let all the contents fall onto the bed. It was not a small fortune.

There were gold necklaces and rings and bangles, all huddled within the square container. And then there were the gold coins, with images of various deities embossed on each one of them. There were also a few coloured precious stones like ruby and emerald, all laid out randomly upon each other.

It was true. The Patriarch had indeed been as enterprising as prudential.

They were all smiling and Uttaran and Suma gave a tight hug to their parents and Uncle. Uttaran went out to the living room. The workers were busy with their duties. He looked up to the heavens, closed his eyes and gave a silent thanks in prayer.

He had a load of finishing works to complete now.

He had gathered the workers and told them that they would be paid well if they completed all remaining works by evening itself. The workers gladly complied and briskly went about their jobs, a couple of them refilling the hole while the others had carefully begun to mount the new replacement slab over the filled hole. The Slab was placed over the exact spot and finally grouted. The Tulsi plant had been delicately re-potted into the recessed space at the top of the slab. By next morning, the slab would take grip firm and strong.

The look of the slab was old and weathered, but even then, one could easily make out that it was not the original slab if looked at closely. But no one would. No one had the time and inclination to walk over and observe the fine intricacies that a stone slab held.

It was beginning to get dark now. Uttaran and Suma called to the workers once all the works were completely finished, and the patch up works entirely done. All the rubble was cleared from the courtyard corner and cleaned up. They handed over a thick wad of notes to the head worker and asked him to distribute it evenly amongst themselves. The workers seemed to be happily content with it and thanked the siblings heartily and departed, no doubt to enjoy a good round of country drinks and finish it off with some nice grand dinner. They were not quite sure what had just happened, but they were very clear that the residents had been extremely pleased with their job.

It was late night now and both siblings were famished. They sat down at the dining table where dinner was ready to be served. The parents and Uncle were already seated. The smiles on their glowing faces said everything. The talk centred round their great luck and fortune, and how they would divide and distribute the rich findings amongst Mother's siblings. Uttaran was already deliberating about how he could resign from his job and settle in the town nearby, a move that would keep him close to his parents and also fulfil his dream of living a slow, albeit peaceful life, allowing him to pursue his whims and fancies liberally. Suma clearly had no such intentions and decided she would carry on with her life just the way it had always been. The parents had always been accustomed to a simple lifestyle and the recent developments would not have too much impact on their lives.

It had been a long and exhausting day and they all went to sleep immediately after dinner.

The next morning, Uttaran was up, but a bit late. The others were already at the dining table for breakfast. They were having the regular banter about how spicy the chutney was, and how tangy the sambar. He smiled at them, walking past and ahead to the bathroom.

He splashed his face a couple of times and stared into the mirror. His mind was completely blank and there was no hint of frenzy in his mind. All was calm. He quickly brushed his teeth and joined the others at the table.

The accomplishment of such a feat had still not sunk in.

After breakfast, the parents and Uncle were once again jovially discussing about how the spoils would be shared, and whether the sisters would get more of the bounty than the brothers, just in jest. There was enough for everyone and each sibling would get its full and equal share.

Such bounties, especially the serendipitous ones, came with their own perils. When one tried to take wrong advantage and covet anothers' rightful share, such events, ironically, had even led to endless and irreversible misfortune in families due to infighting and squabbles over who deserved more. It was best to dutifully share the find in equal, and follow through just like the Patriarch would have wanted.

After all, anyone could have come upon the bounty. And it was only fair that all the other rightful owners should get their equal share in the findings.

Uttaran had moved to the Patriarch's old sleeper chair, now polished and gleaming timber brown. He laid back loosely and stretched his legs out to lay them on one of the extended armrests. He was looking at the main big hall on the opposite, the grand space which was used to welcome and seat the guests of the mansion. It was a wide enclosure with three walls and open to the courtyard in front, so that the hall was entirely visible from any portion of the house. There were rows of strong antique wooden chairs that were still in use, all polished and well maintained. On the walls were some paintings, old and faded, and a couple of decorative deer and bull heads on the walls facing each other, made from wood and intricately detailed. In the centre of the middle wall hung a huge painting of the Grand Patriarch. The painting had always been there ever since Uttaran could remember, never moved and never tampered with. It was a very old original with only the Grand Patriarch, dressed in simple traditional attire and wearing a pair of circular steel rimmed spectacles, seated on the very same sleeper chair that Uttaran was resting on. No smiles, but just stoically glaring.

He could hear the banter going on in the living room, and a lady worker was going about her cleaning chores of the mansion. Uttaran was not thinking about anything in particular, staring blankly at it.

And then, he again had a flash. A weird one.

What if the Patriarch had another hidden bounty? A second hidden treasure.

There was a possibility that either one, or even both of the treasures, were never to be found, let alone even be considered about. What then, if the Patriarch had devised a two-way solution? One bounty, substantial, and hidden away so that it could not be discovered easily and inadvertently, and the other, slightly lesser portion, tucked away nearby and easier to locate and recover so that the descendants could make do with at least a part of his hard-earned prosperity, if not the full and wholesome.

Uttaran got up from the sleeper chair and walked over to the grand hall and looked at the portrait of the Patriarch. He then looked around in the hall and tried to gauge anything that could be a hideaway spot for a little bounty. The decorative wooden heads of the deer and the bull did strike as likely spots, but there was a clear problem. The decorative heads were very beautiful and attractive, and any descendant, as part of his rightful share, could put claim to these objects and carry them away as their own, unknowingly taking with them riches of the house.

Uttaran looked around, and there seemed to be no other likely hideaway spots in the hall. He walked back slowly, looking at the courtyard and searching for some signs.

He once again rested down on the sleeper chair and closed his eyes, oblivious to the chatter going on. And then, suddenly, he sprang up.

He got up from the chair and turned to look at it closely. The chair, wooden and antique, made from fine timber, was simply designed yet elegant and authoritarian. It was something that could enhance one's clout, and any order directed from such a high seat would carry double the stern. There was a clear distinction between standing and spraying orders to the ordinary, and being seated calm and undisturbed on this grand throne of a seat, as if decreeing judgements to the humble workers standing below, their heads bowed down in reverence.

Uttaran bent down to look under the chair. They were all narrow planks closely and tightly placed together to form a seamlessly flowing back and curvy base of the seat. The chair was supported on four strong legs, decorated with engravings carved into them. Each of the legs had a square base about two inches high, on which they solidly stood. Uttaran tapped the legs of the chair lightly. There was no hollow sound. They were clearly solid throughout. He lifted the chair from the front holding the armrests up and tried to get a close look at the square bases. It was not a whole, single piece that made up the entire leg of the chair. The square base was clearly separate from the upper leg, and had been attached to the lower portion of the leg. He tapped the square base lightly. It sounded hollow. He tapped again. He let the chair down softly and moved to the back of the chair and repeated the same procedure. The legs were solid, but the bases of each of the legs sounded hollow.

He rushed upstairs to get the metal detector he had packed and tucked away in one of the bedrooms. He brought it down, opened the contents, assembled them quickly and switched it ON.

He slowly began to hover the scanning base of the detector near the footings of the chair. As he held the detector to one of the legs at the back, the beeping came on. The pointer had jumped up in the markings. To the exact point where it had jerked during the previous endeavour. Uttaran could not hold his excitement. He called Suma over. He moved the scanning base again and showed the display of the detector. Suma could not believe it either. He looked at the chair, and then turned around to look at his parents and uncle. They too, had gotten up to come and look over.

The detector was beeping hard. Uttaran revealed his apprehensions about some riches probably hidden in the little square bases of the legs of the chair. The bases would have to be removed without causing any damage to them and the legs of the chair. They would require an experienced carpenter familiar with the makings of antique furniture who would be able to dismantle the bases cleanly, and then reattach them with the required delicate expertise without causing any damage to the whole.

This would be a tough nut to crack.

The parents and Uncle were still looking in disbelief. Was it possible that there were two sets of hidden treasures? And both being located within a span of couple of days? It seemed absolutely incredulous.

Uttaran asked Mother to call for a carpenter.

There had always been a family carpenter who would promptly arrive on call from the manor house, assess the requirement of furniture, some of which were very uniquely specific and not the easiest to devise and undertake. For generations down the line, the family had been serving the Manor house. Using the best quality of wood that would not only shine in quality but also come good in span of longevity, and in a timely and professional execution of the project, he would invariably deliver. The ladies of the house were seldom disappointed with the end product, and would make sure that the carpenter was handsomely rewarded for his proficient expertise.

Mother informed that it would be a couple of hours before the carpenter could reach home. He was away on some work in town.

Uttaran was curious as to how such an intricate plan could even be devised and implemented without anyone within the family, or even an outsider for that matter, not being privy to. The Patriarch would have had to discuss such matters with someone at least, and then compulsorily have to convey it to the carpenter who would have the very tempting task of having to hide some precious stones in the base of the chair without letting his inner demons get to the better of him.

Well, probably the carpenter was compensated very well in commensurate with the clandestine mission, so that the secret could never be divulged out of him.

But the Patriarch had to keep at least a single, trusted family member in the loop so that in the event of an untimely departure, there would be someone to pass on the secret of the hidden stones. Either that, or... maybe the Patriarch simply decided to have some fun along the way.

The family discussions stopped abruptly when the carpenter walked in. Uttaran recognised him instantly. The carpenter had been to the house numerous times in the past years. He had grown older but the face was still clearly familiar. He greeted the family with a slight bow and gently enquired as to why he had been called for. He was carrying his tools in an old cloth bag with a frayed sling that was hung over his frail shoulder. His teeth were partly stained by a bloody red, indicating he had just been chewing on a juicy paan leaf.

Mother took him over to the sleeper chair and asked him to check whether the bases of the legs of the chair were hollow. The carpenter bent down and first had a look around the chair, then folded up his lungi and squatted to examine the bases closely. He took out a knocker from his bag and started to tap the bases. Not completely satisfied, he called Uttaran over and asked him to help turn the chair completely over and lay it upside down, with all the four bases up in the air. He then tapped the bases again one by one. He was not convinced they were hollow. However, on Uttaran's insistence, he followed the procedure once again. He had finished with three, and finally, at the fourth base, he tapped.

And then, he tapped again lightly, listening closely with his ear cocked to the base. He kept the knocker down and looked very closely at the joint conjoining the leg to the square base. He went back to the other three and repeated the same procedure, and finally returned back again to the fourth.

The parents were getting anxious now. Suma had moved closer to the chair and observed intently at what the carpenter was doing.

The carpenter turned around and asked for permission to detach the base from the leg. It would not take long and there would be no damage to the chair. The parents and Uncle nodded an okay, and the carpenter briskly went about expertly scooping the base from the leg, while plucking various little tools from his kit bag all the time.

The base was eventually separated from the leg after an arduous effort. The base seemed solid and entirely covered with no signs of any attachments. The carpenter was still closely examining the base, turning it over and over in his hands. He stopped at one point, looked deeply into the leg of the upturned chair, and then tapped the detached base again a few more times. He finally took out a scooper. He felt the surface of the base lightly with his finger and very delicately grazed the scooper over it. He looked at the surface again very closely, examining it now at eye level, with one eye closed.

Very finely, he filed out a few thin slices of layer of the surface and then scooped out a very tiny mould of hardened wood. It was a piece of wood putty that had hardened with time. The carpenter brought the base to the parents and showed them the surface that had just been scooped out. There was a clear recess into the surface and the carpenter, once again, asked for permission to explore further. The parents once again nodded their approval and the carpenter sat down on the floor, with his one foot pressing down on the base securely tight, and began to prod and open out the recess.

A few palpitating moments later, in the hands of the carpenter came out a tightly knotted cloth, bright red in colour, about the size of his fist. He carefully handed over the find to Uttaran's Mother, his eyes wide open in curious amazement as were the others. Uttaran's mother handed over the rounded little ball of cloth to Uncle. The Carpenter too was keenly looking over the shoulders of the family, astonished, and eager to decipher this weird find.

Mother called out to a lady worker inside, and very cordially, asked the family carpenter to be taken inside to the kitchen and be served tea and snacks. Prying eyes were not right for such moments.

Uncle slowly opened out the knot and laid it open carefully on the teapoy. And there they were.

Another set of precious coloured stones and gold coins huddled over each other. Though smaller, they seemed to be even more lustrous and shiny than the previous find of bunch. Maybe there were diamonds too. Mother picked up a handful of the coloured stones up in her hand and looked closely. Amongst the stones were some tiny twinkling ones, diamonds definitely. Uncle and Father too, picked up a couple from the teapoy. Though they did not know too much about precious stones, the red and emerald green hues of the stones clearly announced what they indeed were.

Uttaran was watching all this quietly. Flabbergasted. He turned around to look at the chair, which still lay overturned and the detached leg-base lying nearby. He picked up the square base and examined it. Only the Patriarch could have conjured such an ingenious plan.

No doubt he would have amassed such a fortune during his heydays as an enterprising Landlord, collecting the massive and endless proceeds from the estate and very prudently bartering them for some very precious possessions with the affluent and prosperous merchants of the times.

The parents, meanwhile, advised Uncle to take a few of the stones and visit a couple of reputed jewellers known to them in town and have the stones checked for valuation. But that was for later. Discretion was of the essence now, and allowing spread of news of such serendipity was not always wise.

They called the carpenter back in and asked him to re-attach the base to the leg. The carpenter went about his job and promptly set the attachment with the same finesse so that there was not even the slightest aberration from its original. The job was paid for very generously and the carpenter, implicitly instructed to that none of the proceedings and happenings were to be discussed with outsiders, left the mansion happy and satisfied.

The parents, Suma and Uncle were animatedly discussing about the recent events and how incredulous it all seemed. One had always read about treasures, antiques and riches being unearthed and discovered in various articles in the newspapers, but no one expected it to happen in their own dreary and monotonous lives.

And they had just hit two hot spots in the blink of an eye.

They would have the find appraised and valuated by a professional and then, finally call and apprise the concerned families of the good fortune so that they could come over and take their share of what was rightfully theirs. This part was best left to the elders in the family.

Suma had planned to leave by the overnight bus to Bengaluru. Uttaran meanwhile, after all the eventful happenings in the past couple of days, had decided to extend his stay till the coming weekend. He wanted to savour the thrill and simply laze around, and let the fortuitous state of affairs slowly sink in.

He could hear the distant horn of the train from far beyond. He smiled as he closed his eyes, lying on the sleeper chair.

CHAPTER THIRTEEN

THE PATRIARCH'S STORY

After the young Patriarch had been disowned by his paternal family, allegedly for bringing disrepute and dishonour to the family name, he had decided to leave the village and head for the city. He was heartbroken that he had to leave his young sister behind, but he also took comfort in the thought that she would be well-taken care of, by the family. He had no idea where to go and what he would do but somewhere deep down, he knew he would manage. A kind aunt at home had secretly handed over some money and food to him when he had been asked to leave the family home. He thanked her from his heart, taking it as a blessing from her. He realised that her blessings would help him brave the unknown. Somehow, he found the strength to go on, knowing that some kind soul would be praying for him. And he was determined to return and take his sister back with him.

After spending his first night in the city under the open night sky, he decided to head for the docks where the ships arrived for loading and unloading of the cargo. He approached a few people and finally, one kind fellow decided to hire him. He was ready to do any work and took up all sorts of odd jobs at the harbour, all the time looking for and planning to tap some avenue that would better his future. He finally landed a job at the harbour canteen where despite the hard and grinding work routine, he was assured of food all three times of the day. This in turn helped in that, whatever little earnings he had, he was able to save almost the whole of it.

Born with an aptitude that allowed him to seek his goals while overcoming obstinate obstacles and situational hurdles as if they weren't even there, he stubbornly refused to acknowledge the presence of any hardships and just kept going. All that he could very clearly see was a vision of himself back at his village, seated on a chair under the shaded porch of his home and looking at the green paddy fields stretching far and beyond, all his.

When his minuscule corpus just about had gathered a bit, and given his enterprising nature and head brimming full with ideas, he finally managed to secure a small loan from a few of his friends and opened a small tea and breakfast shack in the vicinity of the harbour. With the consistent quality of the home cooked flavours, the humble shack soon turned to a little restaurant that was soon to become the favourite joint for most of the dock workers. He was able to quickly repay all his debts. Fortune smiled on him further and the venture instantly proved to be a winning success. Still restless and not content with this initial burst, his high ambitions and vision of a grandeur lifestyle pushed him on as the Patriarch went on to open a few more such restaurants, and through sheer zeal and sweat and hard work, amassed a substantial fortune in a very short period.

In time, he had also got married and had been blessed with a happy little family.

He also was gracious enough to employ some of his friends from the docks, many of whom had struggled with him during his initial days of hardships while forging unbreakable bonds of friendship and loyalty. This was his humble way of showing deep acknowledgement of all the acts of help and kindness he had received during his hard days at the docks.

Alongside, the continuous stream of customers resulted in the far and rippling spread of his circle of friends and acquaintances, and he made sure he maintained and kept in regular touch with the contacts as they would come very handy in his future endeavours.

He had now quickly grown popular in local circles due to his entrepreneurship and social skills, and harboured deep ambition to align closely with the high and powerful Lords of the times, realising very early that proximity to the High-Standing and Powerful entities and staying put in their good books would ensure instant prosperity and fortune.

In no time, he had come in close ranks with those in the higher echelons in society. His acts of charity were ample and had begun to get noticed and noted. And as he gradually showcased and proved his skilful organisational capabilities and mettle in the high societies, he was duly rewarded in kind.

The most fortuitous rewards were the ones where land estates in the deep interiors of villages were handed over to the Patriarch to overlook, and to be responsible for the tax revenue sourced from those inaccessible and neglected regions.

As he found himself overly occupied with the daily management of affairs of developing the hinterland estates, the Patriarch realised the true hidden worth of these undeveloped lands. The soil was rich and fertile and there were a couple of streams running through the area. If planned rightly, there were vast tracts of heaths that could be used for cultivating crops throughout the year. The water could be diverted to irrigate these lands during the non-monsoons. This would result in humongous output and produce from the estate. The densely forested hills in the surroundings, he would not bother for now. But he could always randomly plant saplings of timber and other hard wood to further afforest the area and its surroundings. The workforce would not be too much of a problem. There were the local villagers whom he could gather.

Foreseeing very lucrative returns if determined and persevered effort was put in consistently there, he gradually withdrew himself from the restaurant business in the city, handing them over completely to a couple of his capable subordinates, some of whom had been very close friends of his at the docks. Even though the Patriarch refused to partake any of the proceeds, the grateful friends strongly insisted and made sure that some part of the profits was passed on and handed over to the Patriarch regularly.

After a couple of years had passed since his duties as a landlord, The Grand Patriarch had proved himself duly with sizeable tax revenues, and had also assured the higher lords of an increased revenue by explaining to them how he could transform the non-arable lands and was planning to extract the maximum output if he was given a free hand to govern over the estates. And impressed by his supreme confidence and feasibility of his grandiose designs, the High Vassal of the region himself agreed to let him undertake complete administration of the hinterlands.

The Grand Patriarch had free reign over about 250 acres of village lands now scattered all over, some plain lands and some in the hilly terrains, and some totally inaccessible. He gathered a few of the local villagers, and from amongst the elders in the group, he selected four of the most prudent and discussed with them a few urgent matters. Over the days, he decided to appoint them as subordinates who would travel, communicate and convey his urgent plans to the people in all the villages under his gaze. Although initially, the villagers were apprehensive about the motives of their new Landlord as they had been of all others before him, but gradually, with the passing of time, the villagers were eventually convinced and gathered in full support of the Patriarch and rallied behind him in all his endeavours.

The Patriarch, on his part, promised that he would make sure that the villagers and the lands under him would thrive in prosperity. He was now responsible for all of them, and for the villagers he was their sole benefactor. He would take care of all their needs and problems. They were all now a part of his extended family.

Through steely determination, he had undertaken this mammoth of a mission, and given the limited resources at hand, truly seemed an impossible and daunting horizon to achieve.`

Prioritizing the primary requirements of the majority of the local villagers who inhabited the few villages under his governance, he first and foremost undertook mission to make sure that water for irrigation reached all the arable fields so that beyond the monsoons, the fields would still remain cultivable for the rest of the whole year. This would optimize the yield of the lands. For this to be achieved, narrow water channels were dug out from the earth and routed to the lands from the nearest water sources. The running brooks and a stream were the perennial water sources there, which were diverted at a few points of their run and utilised to form small water reservoirs.

Many of the uneven heaths and wild-shrubbery filled tracts were levelled plain and further added to the land bank of the topography so as to maximise arability. And those vast tracts that were closest to and bordered the water sources were planted with coconut saplings. They would grow unhindered with such proximity to the water soaked earth beneath. Banana plantains were planted in hordes as they grew wild and undeterred in such conducive and harmonious climatic conditions. They would also provide the natural shade for the young saplings of other crops. Pepper and other such creepers were laid out in between the rows of the arecanut saplings. Cashew trees were already present scattered in the many tracts and they were left untouched for the valued cashew kernels as well as for the fenny produce from the sour juice of the fruit. They would come plenty in handy when the tired workers would refresh and regale themselves with evening tales accompanied by hordes of the local fenny.

Alongside all this, the Patriarch garnered ambition for a residential Mansion, a sort of a Manor house from where he could supervise, monitor and govern the entire estate. He had selected a vast tract of land, slightly uneven, and higher up in level from the surrounding lands.

It was a perfectly natural high seat for a Grand Mansion.

The tract would have to be cleared and levelled further to create a heath, unobstructed and free. The tract was strategically located. It was not too far from the running stream so water would never be a problem for the residence. He would employ most of the workers from the fields and salvage whatever wood and timber that would be left from the clearing of the tract. He would have to plan prudently to utilise all resources to the optimum, and could not let anything go to waste. Remuneration to the workers could be managed by providing them with their daily quota of rice and vegetables that could be sourced from the paddy fields. They could also be pacified by allotting to them spaces for their hutments, which would allow for quick to-and-fro routines with regards to the mansion work site.

The Patriarch had arranged a stone-laying Puja ceremony attended by a very small gathering of close family and had immediately initiated the project.

The most gruelling part was the clearance of the land spread which would house the main residential portion of the mansion. It was March ending, and the hot season had just begun. The workers toiled hard in the sun, their dark skins sweating profusely and glistening while they went about tirelessly, hacking the wild shrubbery with their sharp sickles. They had to also be careful about the reptiles lurking in the dense undergrowth. Every now and then, rat snakes and even cobras, would suddenly spring out from nowhere and dart away in the blink of an eye. The workers would break only for lunch. After a short rest under the shades of the rustling trees, they would once again get back to the toil. Even the lady workers would join them to give a helping hand. The ladies would then head back to their hutments at around 4PM and collectively prepare tea and some snacks, and then return so that the workers in the field could refresh themselves with a short break under the cooling shades of the few cashew trees that stood unharmed in the vast tract. The work then went on non-stop till 6.30PM, after which the workers had been very strictly instructed to stop work and retire to their hutments.

All through the entire routine, the Patriarch, along with a couple of elderly workers, would direct them with abrupt shouts, most of the while standing under an umbrella held by a loyal alongside. The evening deadline was a strict stop as the nearby forests were home to a few wild animals, and one could not risk attack from them so as to not frighten the workers away from the place permanently.

As so it went, day after day, month after month, for a few years. The express development of the land estate and the mansion project advanced together side by side simultaneously. Obstacles there were many but to the Grand Patriarch, it was just another challenge to overcome. This innate character of his, to overcome any hurdle determinedly, was his primary source of strength. It helped to inspire and reinvigorate the workers and the villagers and to put in their best efforts towards whatever cause they were working at. They were completely convinced that all the relentless efforts they were putting would finally result in great benefits of their own in the near future.

Slowly, but surely, the entire estate was transformed into a vast spread of green paddy fields, interspersed and surrounded by plantations of coconut and arecanut and banana plantains. There were also several tracts of land close to the hillocks which had been left untouched and dense with trees of timber and naturally growing wild shrubbery.

And finally, after staying determinedly resolute throughout the progress of the mission, the day finally came when dawn fell on the completed marvel.

It was a day of great rejoice when all the close kith and kin had gathered together to celebrate the grandest of all house-warming ceremonies. All the gathered ones were in awe of this mansion, a vision of such grandeur and yet so very flawless in execution. The magnificent view of the front of the mansion which had a vast, lush green paddy field and the waves of gently swaying green tops of the recently planted coconut and arecanut saplings just beyond was literally breath taking. And now, within a year, the plantations would start yielding their produce. The running stream was a perennial source of water and water would never be a problem at the estate.

The rich rice produce from the numerous paddy fields had always been in large surplus. It was more than sufficient to keep the little army of workers content, and as a result, the entire estate was in a state of happy self-sustenance. This precisely, had been the primary goal of the Patriarch. To develop an estate that would run and sustain itself in clockwork precision, and which would require nothing more than a frequent dosage of supervision and monitoring. The regular care and upkeep was completely ensured by the abundance of farm hands permanently dwelling in the estate. He also made sure that the necessities and everyday needs of the workers and their families who had stood by him for all these years were fulfilled satisfactorily.

Slowly, as the years went by and as the family grew, the Patriarch had amassed great wealth. Blessed with endless prosperity, he had even visited his paternal home, as he had promised to himself. He had taken with him a good amount of riches which he had handed over to the family. He harboured no ill towards any of them. He fondly, and with great gratitude, remembered how the kind aunt had helped him when he had to leave home with nothing, and nowhere to go.

He also brought back his young sister, now a widow and with a young daughter, to stay in his new mansion.

His mission was now complete and fulfilled.

As time went by, he had finally come to work on a plan to secure the riches for himself and his descendants who would follow. Not only for them, but he also wanted to ensure a good life for the future generations that would emerge down the line. He had also lined up a plan for his sister, who had nowhere to go and no one to call her own. He would make doubly sure that she would never be in want. He had always doted on his little sister right from their childhood, and he could never bear to see her in trouble or pain ever again.

The immovable property, though difficult, would be relatively easy to divide and demarcate as inheritance amongst the inheritors. The major portion of the estate and the whole mansion, he would pass on to his sister. His sons could have the large developed estates in the surrounding villages. They could stay in the mansion till the time they were around, but after them, the sole proprietary rights of the mansion would belong exclusively to his sister. And after her, to her only daughter.

It seemed harsh to his sons and their respective families, but the Patriarch was headstrong and would not have it any other way.

But the real problem would be dividing the gold and jewellery and the precious stones and gems that the Patriarch had collected and amassed.

He had, over the years, bartered the humongous surplus from his estates with the rich merchants for precious stones and gold. The rice produce and arecanuts, along with the pepper, had always been in huge never-ending demand, and merchants were always ready to trade their hard-gained riches for these valuable commodities. The Patriarch, in this manner, had amassed a large fortune in the form of precious stones and gold.

Going about planning to divide this large fortune was a major problem now.

It would lead to disruption in the joint family if not undertaken rightly. So much wealth inherited overnight would make anyone's mind and soul go wild. After giving it a lot of hard thought, he finally decided that after the division of part of the riches, he would hide away some part of the fortune, not only to ensure sanity and unity in the family but also to ensure that all the hard-earned wealth is not entirely wasted, and there would be something to fall back on during the unforeseen and difficult times.

After some deep contemplation, he finally decided on the perfect spot to hide the riches. He would mark a spot in the central courtyard and bury it deep underground, after securing the riches in a hardy container or box so as to ensure the contents do not get damaged by soil or weather. He would mark the spot by relocating the TULSI SLAB from the centre and grouting it over the hiding spot. And then, a flash of genius. Why not hide the compact container in the base of the TULSI SLAB itself? No one would ever tamper with the sacred slab and it would provide as the perfect marker. And no one would ever sense a whiff unless he revealed it. He would leave a hint of the location. Something subtle, that would be evident to the searching and curious eye.

He would commission a portrait of himself and in the portrait, he would leave a clue that would lead one to the secret in the Tulsi slab. He would also leave a clue for the little bounty that he planned to hide away in his favourite sleeper chair. It would be in the very small inscription at the bottom of the painting.

Tulsi Volagge Kursi Kelagge (in Kannada, meaning Inside the Tulsi, under the chair).

The Patriarch seemed to be enjoying the whole exercise now. He had lived a full life, and it was time for some fun now.

He also planned to hide a surprise within the silver container box to be hidden in the TULSI SLAB. He would carve out a secret compartment within the box and stash a few more precious gems, just for the fun of it. Let's see who gets them. He was grinning mischievously now.

THE END

www.ingramcontent.com/pod-product-compliance
Lightning Source LLC
La Vergne TN
LVHW041043150826
845672LV00001B/440

* 9 7 9 8 8 9 3 6 3 6 7 5 8 *